HEART IN THE DESERT, HAND ON THE MESA

Mary S. McCracken

Avid Readers Publishing Group
Lakewood, California

Heart in the Desert, Hand on the Mesa

Avid Readers Publishing Group

http://www.avidreaderspg.com

ISBN-13:978-1-61286-334-4

Printed in the United States

For Opal

HEART IN THE DESERT, HAND ON THE MESA is based on the true experiences of my parents, fictionalized for the sake of story. The names have been changed and some characters invented. The Keresan language has never been a written language so the spellings are only approximate. I have used my father's notes as he struggled to learn the language of the Laguna and Acoma people.

Keresan

Amoo	expression of sympathy
Baba	grandmother
Da-wa-eh	thank you
Dru-we-shots	good bye
Dyety	rabbit
Eh-hiay	exclamation of surprise
Ga-wa-tse	hello
Goo-wa-goo	chicken
Hah	yes
Kenuty	green corn
Naya	mother
Niash-che-uh	father
We-meh	never mind

Seminary Hill, Texas
February 7, 1944

Dear folks,

    I received the letter and check from you and you can't imagine how surprised I was. I was so short on funds that I thought I would have to spend my last semester in Seminary, not in classes, but working wherever I could find employment to replenish my funds. Now I can go ahead and complete my seminary education.

        What next? I am thinking about applying for a chaplaincy in some branch of military service to do my part in the war effort. But I pray the war will soon be over as I'm sure you do as well.

Give my love to all,
Robert

Seminary Hill, Texas
March 10, 1944

Dear folks,

        I have been inquiring into this chaplain business. They say that the quota of protestant chaplains is already filled at present, they are not accepting any more. My counselor, Dr. Summers, says it may only be a few months until it opens up again.

        I've been considering it a long time. I told my pastor my circumstances and how I felt, and he advised me to get my application in at once because it would take some time to get my papers through. Meanwhile I can decide finally whether I will sign on the dotted line or no.

Lots of love,
Robert

Seminary Hill, Texas
March 30, 1944

Dear folks,

I did, in fact, talk with the enlistment official at Fort Worth, and he told me that a chaplain in the military service would be required to practice whatever the commanding officer told him to practice concerning religious services he must perform. He knew some who had been put in very embarrassing situations by the commanding officer.

That settles the question for me, because that seems to me an unacceptable compromise.

I am now thinking something about mission work in West Virginia or Kentucky in the Appalachian communities. Dr. Summers is helping me look into it.

Lots of love,
Robert

Seminary Hill, Texas
April 27, 1944

Dear folks,

I am now working on my last term paper. Soon that will be all over forever. I don't believe I could be sorry if I had to! Term papers always did rub me the wrong way.

I am glad you have heard from Sam. What did he say? I haven't heard from him in a long time.

I have been notified by Brother Stumph that the mission work appointments have been made and I am to work south of Albuquerque, New Mexico on the Laguna Indian reservation.

Brother Stumph says my work will be mostly preaching and altogether with the Indians.

The work looks more and more interesting, but difficult. Pray for me.

Love to all,
Robert

ONE

JUNE 6, 1945
Santa Fe, New Mexico

"Mayonnaise, no cheese."

"Pardon?" Minna Cagle turned her good ear to the conductor.

"*Buenas noches, Senorita.* Welcome to Santa Fe."

"Oh. Of course. Grass-see-us, seen yore." She gratefully accepted the conductor's hand as she stepped off the train.

The acrid odor of the locomotive wafted upward with a cloud of hissing steam. Minna pressed a lemon verbena scented handkerchief to her nose to stave off a wave of nausea. *Law me! Let me off!*

The last time she had traveled by rail, the folks were taking the family to relatives in Chattanooga. She was six years old on that occasion and had spent every mile bent over the toilet bowl. She remembered wondering, as children do, if it was possible to actually cough up one's internal organs. Thankfully she reached their destination before that happened.

This time she had reached Santa Fe before her childhood theory could be further tested. *Not a moment too soon!*

The train station was small but bustling with activity. A whitewashed adobe building with blue doors and terra cotta tiled roof greeted travelers beyond the initial platform. There was a seating area under a flat roof with underlying decorative arches. The building itself had a definite Spanish flavor. It might have been a station somewhere in old Mexico rather than New Mexico. Minna gazed out over a sea of hats and chattering passengers scurrying to find their luggage. Several sweaty bodies bumped her

1

as she was jostled along with the crowd. She kept the handkerchief pressed to her nose.

Minna found her one large suitcase and dragged it toward the waiting area on the side of the building. How would she ever recognize the ride she had been promised to the Laguna pueblo?

Maybe they will recognize me. She thought in that case, perhaps she should lower the handkerchief so that her face was more visible.

A cowboy swaggered past. He was walking a miniature poodle on a leash. Minna stifled a giggle. *Surely he's not my contact!*

She smoothed her rumpled skirt. Catching her reflection in the station window, she adjusted the perky little hat her mother had insisted she wear the day she left home.

Me, a teacher, what a hoot! Minna shook her head in disbelief. How had this happened? She had signed up for "work study" her last year of college. That would earn the last few credits she needed to graduate plus she needed a way to pay off her school loans, which were considerable. She never dreamed they would send her so far from home. *So far from anywhere!*

Her gaze fell upon a newspaper rack.

U.S., BRITAIN, SOVIET UNION, AND FRENCH LEADERS SIGN DECLARATION OF GERMAN DEFEAT!

Minna sighed audibly. *Now if only the war in the Pacific would come to an end!*

A young sandy haired gentleman was making his way through the crowd. He clutched a photograph in one hand and was looking expectantly at each face as he passed. In his other hand he held a sign that read, " MISS CAGLE." His hair was brushed neatly straight back with a slightly receding hairline. Minna noted he was only a couple of inches taller than her five foot six. His pleasant expression and his gold rimmed glasses helped him look approachable.

The sign had obviously been borrowed from the station. Upon closer inspection she saw that it actually read,

MISS CAGLE
NO SMOKING

Glad to see I'm not on fire…

Minna fluttered her hand. The young man approached.

"Miss Cagle?"

"Yes. You are my ride to Laguna?"

"Afred so."

Minna could not place his accent.

"My automobile is none too reliable, Miss Cagle, but I am here to serve. Nice to meet you. I'm Robert Carlisle." He offered a firm hand shake then plopped a very silly straw hat on his head before reaching for her suitcase. He looked more like a farmer than a cowboy.

"Just the one?"

"Yes, I was told to pack light."

She saw from his grimace, as he heaved the suitcase through the station, he didn't think she had achieved it. *Must be all those books.*

He was right about the automobile. It was a dusty brown, two door, 1938 Ford V8 and no, it didn't look very reliable. There were dents and scratches in abundance and a crack creeping across the windshield on the passenger side.

Minna settled in the front seat while Robert heaved the suitcase into the trunk. He ambled to the front of the car and began pushing it backwards laboriously.

Minna rolled down the window and hollered, "You need help with that, Mr. Carlisle?"

Robert shrugged good naturedly. "I don't have a reverse gear right now and can't get one what with the war." He dropped into the driver's side seat and started the engine. It popped and banged and emitted a foul odor. Minna clamped the handkerchief over her nose again.

Robert looked sheepish.

They progressed through the shadowy streets of Santa Fe with many grinding and clunking noises until they arrived at a place called Palace of the Governors. Robert parked the automobile.

Minna noted to her dismay that she had been holding her breath for much of the time. She made a conscious effort to breathe deeply.

3

Robert had not seemed to notice her nervousness. "I hope you don't mind, Miss Cagle, I need to give your landlady a ride back to Laguna as well."

Sure enough, there was an elderly Indian woman making her way to the car. She was no more than five feet tall, a roundish person with bowed legs. When she walked she shifted from side to side. She was holding a large cardboard box and seemed to be in conversation with Mr. Carlisle even before she was within ear shot. Minna nervously tugged at her good ear.

The old woman was surprisingly spry considering her unusual gait. She arrived at the car and her face appeared in the window. She wore her grey hair short and straight with bangs. Her eyes were enormous behind large thick glasses.

Minna felt to be polite she should get out of the car and offer the old woman the front seat, but she couldn't open the door. The woman was standing too close.

"*Naya*, this is Miss Minerva Cagle. Miss Cagle, this is Mrs. Salita," Robert said.

"I go by Minna." She offered her hand out the open window.

Mrs. Salita shifted the box to one hip and squeezed Minna's fingers.

"So pretty," she said. "So pretty."

Mrs. Salita hurried over to the other side of the car. Robert pushed the seat forward and Mrs. Salita and a younger lady climbed into the back seat. The younger woman also had a large box. They balanced them on their laps.

"This is my daughter Gloria," Mrs. Salita announced. Gloria smiled shyly around the box. She was petite and delicate with soft black hair, small even teeth, and intense brown eyes.

Mr. Carlisle and another man were pushing the car backward again.

"...And that is my no account son-in-law, Leon." Mrs. Salita added. Minna tried not to react at this surprising declaration. She observed that the son-in-law was tall and dark, with a slim body, but broad shoulders. He wore his hair in a single ponytail. His hair was longer than Gloria's or Minna's.

4

Once everyone was squeezed in, they were on their way again.

"I promised Leon I would pick up his brother-in-law at the bus station," Robert said.

Minna was feeling overwhelmed and exhausted. *I'm like an old hound dog, too tired to get up off a rusty nail!.* She realized she couldn't say anything since Mr. Carlisle was giving everyone a ride out of kindness. *I shouldn't complain, but I wonder where everyone will fit in this automobile! Especially with those boxes!*

Minna looked out the cracked window at the amazing sunset gathering over the adobe buildings. It seemed to Minna as if the clouds had been spread over the horizon like so much strawberry jam.

Leon's brother-in-law was waiting for them at the curb by the bus station. He was in military uniform. It reminded Minna of her brother Ernest Leigh, serving in the Pacific, and someone else, she dare not think of without a tug at her heart.

The service lad climbed in next to Minna. This placed her on the divide in the seat that allowed one side to be tipped back to load back seat passengers. To move anywhere else would put her uncomfortably close to either Robert or the new young man.

"*Ga-wa-tse,*" the young man said to Mrs. Salita. Mrs. Salita nodded.

"*Ga-wa-tse,*" he said to the others in turn.

Must mean hello. Minna noted sadly the young man smelled to high heaven of liquor. But she lowered the handkerchief, feeling it would be a little too obvious. She fanned herself with it instead which helped a little.

"Whew! It is sure is hot," she murmured.

Leon grasped the soldier's shoulders over the seat. "*Ga-wa-tse,* Roland!" he said, heartily. Roland looked over the back of the seat into the boxes.

"Potterysh. Did you shell any?" he slurred.

Minna tried not to stare. Roland's skin was a more coppery tone than any of the others so far. These were not the first Indians she had ever seen. There had been a Cherokee village not far from her childhood home in the Smoky mountains.

Mr. Carlisle said, "Roland, this is Miss Cagle who has come to give English lessons to the children before school starts in the fall."

"*Ga-wa-tse*, lady," the young man turned back to her.

"How do you do," she said softly.

Mrs. Salita was not as forgiving. "Roland Rosario, you have been drinking!"

"Have not..." A suspicious statement, as he ended it with a burp.

"Yes, you have! We can all smell it! And in front of the Reverend too! Shame on you!"

Reverend? Minna eyed Mr. Carlisle sideways. She found it hard to imagine this soft spoken gentleman preaching a sermon. She was familiar with the preachers back home that liked the sound of their voices so much they aimed to share them at the loudest decibels.

Mrs. Salita closed her eyes and lay folded hands on her ample bosom. "And be not drunk with wine, wherein is excess; but be filled with the spirit," she said piously. "Egyptians 5:18," she added.

Robert cleared his throat and said softly, "I think you mean Ephesians."

"*Hah,* that's what I meant, Efeedshins."

"*Eh hiay,* I'm on leave from da war, *Naya.* If you had sheen what I have, you'd need a drink too. I am not drunk with wine!" Roland smiled impishly. "I do confesh however, to being full of the spiritsh..." He burped loudly.

To Minna's surprise, shy Gloria jumped into the conversation. "Roland, you know my mother threw out her last husband for drinking. She would never touch that stuff even if she did see the war!"

Leon had a different opinion. "The way I see it, Roland is a warrior for the people. We should honor him! If he wants to drink himself pickled it is none of our business!"

Minna squirmed in her uncomfortable seat. *What have I gotten myself into?*

"Yes, sir," Mr. Carlisle interrupted. "I was proud to get this old clunker of a car when I did. Up until then, I was making this trip on a bicycle! I told my friends if I got this car I would make a joyful noise unto the Lord. I learned since that my joke wasn't funny. The noises this car makes are seldom joyful, and I am sorry to say, neither are mine on those occasions!"

What has that to do with anything? Minna looked at Robert, one eyebrow raised.

"Uh oh, would you look at that!" Mr. Carlisle flipped the headlight switch off and on a few times. "Lights out!" He did the same again. "Broken Again! Good thing there is a full moon to get to Laguna by. We should be all right if everyone helps me watch the road."

All grew silent as they strained to see what lay ahead. The first thing Minna noticed was the road sign "VICTORY SPEED 35 MPH." *At that rate, we will be all night getting to Laguna!* She peered into the growing darkness at the shadow of two black mountains. Were they volcanoes? *Extinct* she hoped! The moonlight revealed a flat terrain of nothingness. After a few more miles she observed ankle high scrub-brush and larger bushes. In the darkness they looked like humpbacked people treading toward a sleeping giant rock.

They journeyed on in silence. Minna thought about the earlier disagreement. She wondered if Mr. Carlisle had deliberately shut off the head lights to deflate the argument.

Roland nodded off with his head against the car window, snoring loudly. Minna covered her nose with her handkerchief against his boozy breath. *Law me!*

***

Leaving Minna in Laguna into the care of Mrs. Salita, Robert shuttled Gloria and Leon on to Paguate, then doubled back toward Acomita to take Roland home. Roland had been dozing off on the entire trip.

Robert shifted uneasily in his seat and cleared his throat. He clicked the headlights back on and Roland chuckled.

Noticing that Roland was awake, Robert said gently, "Son, I didn't want to say anything in front of everyone and it is not my intention to shame you, but…" Robert chose his words carefully. "I know you think strong drink helps you forget the horrors of war, but I have seen that it helps many a young man forget something else. That is, how to be who they really are, such as a loving husband, a dutiful son, a faithful friend. When your family sees you like that, they are the ones you are hurting." Robert glanced at Roland who had closed his eyes again. He continued, "They were hoping to have the Roland back that they love and have been missing, not some stranger that the drinking gives them. You will soon be a father. What sort of man do you want your children to think of as their father?"

Roland shrugged but seemed to take no offense. Robert pulled in front of the little adobe house and Roland leaped out before Robert had even brought the automobile to a complete stop. He stumbled and fell into the dust but rolled right back into a standing position.

Robert gasped. "Are you all right?"

Roland nodded. "Thanks for the ride."

Robert saw to it that Roland got inside the house before he made a U-turn in the road and headed back to Laguna with a heavy sigh.

Laguna, New Mexico
June 6, 1945

Hello everyone,

I arrived here safe and sound but I'm pretty sleepy tonight. It took much longer than I anticipated to get to Laguna. I came to Santa Fe by way of Chicago because they said I could get a better connection that way. If that is so, the other way must be a fright!

They call Chicago the melting pot of the world and I can agree. By the time I finally got to Santa Fe, I felt thoroughly melted.

But I am here in Laguna at last, and I expect to get down to work sometime next week.

Laguna is very picturesque, at least what I could see of it in the dark. The houses are all made of the adobe mud. It looks like what I imagine the town of Bethlehem would be like, from the Bible stories. I have a nice place to stay, in one of these houses next door to the schoolhouse.

Maybe when I get rested a little better from the trip, my noggin will clear up and I can write you more about everything.

I've just remembered what it was I forgot to bring. My ration books! Maybe you better send them to the Albuquerque address they said to use for our mail.

I hope I made the right decision coming here. Right now I am feeling overwhelmed and uncertain how to even begin what I was contracted to do.

All for now, I miss you all more than I can say.
Minna

***

Laguna, New Mexico
June 6, 1945

Dear David,

I was exhilarated almost to the point of flabbergastation to get your letter. It's always so refreshing to hear from you, first hand and not through the feminine screenings of our sisters.

I am glad to hear the hay is jumping along and the other crops are doing well. I'd sure love to be there and help you store some of it away. It is surprising what they can get to grow out here in the desert. Mostly corn, beans, squash, and pretty good melon.

So, you think my Indian friends would like me to go girl struck? Well, I'm glad there's still one person anyway who thinks there might be a chance for me. I shouldn't have told you about their teasing. Now you think I don't want to come home. I don't

9

know about that, so maybe I've got a girl and don't know about that either. As for getting married, I couldn't do that. Nobody has asked me yet! But long as I can't come home, it might be a good idea to pitch a little woo to keep from dying of dry rot, don't you think?

Seriously, don't it occur to you that two brilliant, charming, and handsome pole cats like you and me ought to give the members of the fairer sex a break?

I must say, after much teasing, I was especially surprised when I picked up the new "schoolmarm" at the train station today. She is not at all what I expected. In fact, she is quite lovely. She has dark brown hair and big soft blue eyes. I am looking forward to getting to know her better.

Remember what I said, and I want to hear of you stepping out occasionally.

I'll close with the latest my good friend Albert told me here at Laguna:

"Did you hear about the fight down at the barn? …The cat licked his paw."

I'll be seeing you some of these days, I hope.

Your shortest brother,

Robert

TWO

Yus sapish-tu-ra. Tsa-tse nya-we schumano.
(The Lord is my shepherd. I shall not want.)

Before Minna opened her eyes, she smelled strong coffee and fresh baked biscuits. In that sleepy place that she was, she thought she was home. Then she remembered.

She had been so exhausted when they came to Mrs. Salita's the night before that she hadn't even unpacked yet.

Minna rummaged through her suitcase and found a skirt and blouse and tied her hair back with a scarf. She noticed in dismay that a hole was working its way through the sole of her right shoe. No money for shoes for quite a while! Every cent possible had to be used against the school loan.

Minna pulled a shoebox out of her suitcase and emptied it of its contents: her brother Ernest Leigh's pencil drawings of the Smoky Mountains, their childhood home; a photograph of the whole family taken just before he left for military service; and the only photo she had of Ernest Leigh's best friend, Frank, looking so handsome in his military uniform!

She had known Frank since she was a teenager. He and Ernest Leigh had gone through basic training together. She knew he used to think of her as his best friend's goofy little sister. Things had changed when she was in college. She always included a note for him when she wrote to Ernest Leigh. Sometimes Frank would write back with a joke or a story about Ernest Leigh. He asked about her life and her family. He said he missed her.

When the boys went off to war things got more serious. Frank told her secret things that he had not told anyone else. He told her what should become of his things should he not return.

Minna touched the photo of Frank remembering the day he and Ernest Leigh left together, shipping out to war. She got a nice brotherly kiss from Ernest Leigh, who had never kissed her before in his life! Frank shook hands with every one of the family, then ushered her behind her father's truck.

"I want you to have this, Minna." He gave her a silver brooch in the shape of an angel. Minna drew her breath in sharply.

"It was my grandmother's. She would have been pleased to have you keep it safe for me while I'm away." His eyes lingered on Minna's face. He brushed a tear from her cheek as she laid it against his hand. It filled her heart with sadness and longing but surprisingly, also with hope.

"Until we meet again," he said so tenderly she wouldn't have heard him if she had not been concentrating on his handsome face.

Then he had kissed her so earnestly she had to step back to keep her heart from pounding right out of her chest.

Minna shook off the memory as she propped each of the photos against the wall on top of the dresser. She touched her fingertips to her lips then let them pause briefly on the brooch she had attached to her hat. She tore off a piece of the cardboard box to push into her shoe. It would have to "make do."

**

Mrs. Salita spooned grounds into the percolator pot and set it on the cast iron stove. She placed another pan of biscuits in to brown, shook her head as if remembering, then spooned a few more measures into the pot. A mischievous smile played across her face.

She found herself singing as she wiped down the plastic table cloth with a wet rag. *I haven't felt this happy since before Gloria left home to marry that no account Acoma boy, Leon.* The house had seemed impossibly big and lonesome since Gloria left. It was good to have someone to share it again.

Yes, this could all work out. Mrs. Salita smiled to herself. Sure, Minna was supposed to be staying just for the summer, but

Mrs. Salita had other plans, and she had influence. What would be the harm in suggesting to the council that Miss Cagle's contract extend into the fall as a permanent teacher?

Such a pretty young thing! Maybe the reverend would fall in love with her and that would be a good thing too. *Like the good book says in that first book...the book of Geniuses, I think it is... "And the Lord God said, It is not good that man should be alone; I will make him a help meet for him."*

Mrs. Salita adored Reverend Carlisle and fretted over his loneliness. She wanted to be sure he had reason to stay for a good long time to come. He was so like her oldest son, soft spoken and thoughtful. His name had also been Robert. He had gone to war and not come back. Sometimes in church services Robert sounded so like her son she had to take out her handkerchief to dab her eyes.

The coffee began to sputter and pop as she started the eggs. She thought she heard stirrings from the next room. *Good! She is awake! This is going to be fun!*

***

"Good morning," Mrs. Salita met Minna in the kitchen with a mug of strong coffee. "I hope you like it black. I am out of milk. There is sugar if you want, on the table."

I'll say! Minna tried not to make a face as she sipped from the mug. Chicory! It tasted something like burnt tires and skunk essence! She slipped a spoonful of sugar in and then another and another when Mrs. Salita wasn't looking. She made a mental note to ask her folks to mail her ration of coffee grounds.

The table had been set for four places.

"My daughter is coming to get my grocery list. Robert offered to take them to the store. Is there anything you would like me to have them bring back?"

Tea, perhaps!

The front door banged as Gloria and Leon came through. They were arguing in Keresan, their native language, but stopped abruptly when they saw Minna. They joined her at the table. There

13

were scrambled eggs with green chilies, plenty of tomatoes; red, green, and yellow, and the best biscuits Minna had ever tasted.

After they had eaten Leon announced, "Robert should be up by now. You want me to go get him?"

"*We-meh*, never mind." Mrs. Salita said. "Miss Cagle will go. She needs to see her classroom."

Thus dismissed, Minna slipped out the screen door and breathed in the morning air. The sun was still low in the sky as Minna left Mrs. Salita's. The adobe houses glistened in the soft haze over the village. The streets were not paved, just dust and more dust. *What a beige world!* Minna's feet crunched gravel as she approached the building next door.

The old school building was a sight! Most of the plaster was chipping off and the adobe bricks showed through. The windows were caked with dust and there were sand drifts against the door. It looked like brown sugar snow.

OWOOOooooooh. Minna heard the mournful howl of a wounded animal. She tapped on the window and called softly, "Reverend?"

She heard scuffling and a loud crash, more scuffling and then the door creaked open.

Reverend Carlisle's face appeared in the opening. Without his glasses, his eyes were a clear sky blue. His hair was all disheveled and there was a cobweb dangling from a cowlick.

"Miss Cagle, good morning!" He opened the door wide so that she might enter.

"Good morning Reverend."

"Please Miss Cagle, we don't stand on formality here. Just call me Robert. The children do."

OWOOOOooooooh.

Robert cocked his head. "Oh, that." He opened the door wider. "That's just coyotes. You will hear them pretty often here in New Mexico."

As if in answer, several village dogs started barking.

Minna peeped around the room in dismay. It was not at all what she had expected. Cracked walls surrounded one large table; a stack of wooden folding chairs, and a makeshift pulpit.

14

"As you can see, Miss Cagle, it is certainly a multi-purpose room. I promise you I won't be exhibiting my laundry in this fashion when you require the room for your lessons." He hurried across the room and snatched a shirt and several pair of men's under shorts off the privacy curtain pole. His portion of the room looked like a cross between a camping cabin and a hospital room. It held only a single iron bed, a dresser, and a buck stove.

He noticed her gaze at the grimy windows. "I was just about to dust."

"You just bit the dust?" Minna turned her good ear to Robert.

"I realize it still needs a good cleaning. The dust is a constant problem here. You know we call the dust storms 'New Mexico rain'. I'm *afred* the windows aren't exactly air tight..."

"Where are the desks for the children?" Minna dared to ask.

"Oh, there aren't any desks, but you are welcome to use these chairs from the mission." Robert indicated the stack of wooden folding chairs in the corner. "I hold services here Sunday mornings and sometimes Wednesday night, but otherwise I will try to stay out of your way whenever you need the room." His eyebrows raised. "Er...when will you need the room?"

Minna tugged on her good ear. "I'm not sure. I'm expecting someone from the school board to give me some direction. I'm not even sure how the children will know to come."

"Oh, that's no problem, I sometimes have Bible stories for the children in the village. I just go through the streets making noise and they come out of curiosity. Why don't you come over about dusk this evening? I'll show you what I do."

"Thank you, Robert. I'll do that."

They heard Mrs. Salita's screen door slam next door.

"I believe Leon and Gloria are expecting you," Minna offered.

Robert hastily ran his hands through his hair and departed leaving Minna alone in the schoolroom. She unfolded one of the chairs and sat down shakily. Folding her hands in her lap and gazing around the room at her new surroundings, she sighed deeply.

Law me!

The school board representative had still not arrived by evening. Minna decided to try to find Robert in the village. It was very warm. She dabbed at her upper lip with her handkerchief. *Whew!* Shadows were forming east of every dwelling. At least it was almost comfortable in the shade.

As she ventured up the dusty road, she thought she heard the sound of music coming from somewhere up ahead. When she had come to the very center of the village there was a large cottonwood tree. It was shedding its milky white fluff in a much appreciated breeze. It looked like so many fairies flitting about. *How enchanting!* Robert sat under the tree amongst a gathering crowd of mostly children. He was playing an ukulele and was singing in a passable tenor:

> *"He-su shku-wa-tsi-mu*
> *Tsi-dya-tra-nyi shkuh-be-t*
> *E-utr ho-ba sia giash*
> *She sia ho-bah gia-truk."*

Minna recognized the tune as "Jesus Loves Me, This I Know."

> *"Hah, shku wa tsi mu*
> *Hah, shku wa tsi mu*
> *Hah, shku wa tsi mu*
> *Tsi-dya-tra nyi shkuh bet."*

"Everyone," Robert did an ukulele fanfare. "I am pleased to introduce the new summer teacher, Miss Cagle."

Minna felt all eyes fall on her and momentarily got the all overs. Some of the children whispered to each other but they were smiling.

"Miss Cagle, would you like to say anything?"

She tried to think of something fitting but found herself opening and closing her mouth without anything much coming out. *I must look just like a chicken after a worm!*

Then it came to her…

"I wish I had a rooster," she began singing softly.

"A rooster is a very good pet…" she sang a little louder.

"He would wake me in the morning," she sang nice and loud.

"When I've overslept!
ER ER ER ER ER ER ERRRRRR!" Minna crowed.
ER ER ER ER ER ER ERRRRRR!"

The children broke into giggles.

"*Goo-wa-goo*!" some of them shouted.

Robert joined in with the crowing and eventually all the children did as well.

"ER ER ER ER ER ER ERRRRR!"

"Now don't give me a roasting hen…" Minna continued in her best chicken voice.

"A live chicken is what I beg…
If I get too hungry…
She'll give me an egg!
BWAK buk buk buk buk buk buckeeee!
BWAK buk buk buk buk buk buuuuuck!"

By now all the children were clucking or crowing and the adults were smiling. Minna glanced at Robert who winked in approval.

***

"Robert, you certainly can do some unexpected things." Minna imitated the ukulele playing. They walked back toward the school building and Mrs. Salita's house.

"Oh, just a little something I picked up at college. You have some interesting, er, talents yourself." Robert tried his version of the chicken voice.

They both laughed.

"The children are delightful. Thank you for introducing me," Minna said warmly.

"Yes, well. Guess I didn't know much to tell them. Where are you from Minna?"

"East Tennessee, originally from the Smokey Mountain area. I am a bonafide hillbilly!"

They both laughed.

Robert cleared his throat. "Guess the same could be said of me. I am from rural Virginia."

"You don't sound like it." *Except for that 'afred' thing.*

"Nor do you Miss Cagle."

Minna was suddenly reminded of her school years. "I guess our English teachers did a thorough job of beating the dialect out of us."

"Pert' near."

They laughed again. It was a comfortable feeling thinking of home. How she wished she was still there!

"You still have family in Tennessee?" Robert asked.

"Yes. My folks are still there. I have a sister in secondary school, the twins are still in grammar school, and I have an older brother serving in the Pacific war. It is very hard to get any information on where he is." *Or where Frank is…*

"I will keep him in my prayers."

Maybe that will mean something, coming from a reverend!

"Thank you Robert." What of your family?"

"One brother, back from the war, stationed at Dalhart, Texas. The other has taken over the responsibility of the farm since my father passed. I have two sisters still living at home. One is a teacher like yourself."

Minna ducked her head, chuckling. "Oh, I don't really think of myself as a teacher yet, more as an assistant. I was hired just to prepare the children a little before the real school year begins."

"You'll find some of them know very little English. That seems true among the very young and the very old here in Laguna. Most of the people our age went to Indian school in Santa Fe as youngsters where they were forced to learn English."

"Forced?"

"Yes, *afred* so. They don't like to talk about it."

Minna could relate. She recalled her painful school experience as a young student in the Smokey Mountains. She was reprimanded with a ruler each time she said, "Ain't." She shuddered at the memory.

"How horrible!" Minna exclaimed. She stumbled over a dip in the road and Robert grabbed her arm to steady her.

18

When she had composed herself, she asked, "How did you end up in Laguna, Robert?"

Robert gazed up at the turquoise sky and smiled. "I have the honor of reopening the work that was begun by Samuel Gorman in 1849. It was pretty much abandoned after he left. You see the Indian Council is predominantly Catholic, but they recently agreed to let us lead those of the Protestant persuasion here in Laguna. There is a Presbyterian preacher over at Paguate but he never holds services here. Mostly I just try to help out wherever I see the need. The Laguna people are a very friendly tribe and they make it easy to be their friend."

"It must be a real challenge, living like you do. No running water or electricity."

"A challenge, yes. Hauling water is no problem now that I have the toodlelooka."

"The toodle-what?" Minna turned her good ear to Robert.

"The toodlelooka. It's what the children call my automobile. That's the way the horn sounds to them, I guess. It has certainly been a blessing to have transportation. I wouldn't be much good balancing water pots on my head as the women do here." He stopped and lifted one shoulder in thought. "I have learned that some blessings come with problems as well." Robert shrugged and continued his walk. "The toodlelooka has constant breakdowns, but I guess that is common with most vehicles these days."

Minna thought of the bare room Robert was occupying. "You use the buck stove to heat water?"

"Oh, I try not to in the summer. It heats up the room too much. I use an ordinary kerosene lamp to heat water for shaving and washing, and I can even warm canned soups by suspending a pot from the ceiling by a string."

"That's amazing! Very inventive of you."

Robert laughed. "I am sometimes too inventive for my own good. The first time I attempted that, I tried to heat a can of turnip greens and after enjoying that first meal, long before daylight I was suffering nausea and worse all the rest of that night. The next day was to be my first church service there in the school building. I was so weak, weary and uncomfortable, I had to do the best I could, preaching from a sitting position!"

19

"Law me! How did that go over?"

"Guess my congregation thought I was in need of a pulpit. That's when they presented me with the one I use now." Robert had reached Mrs. Salita's door. He opened it for Minna. "Well, here we are. Let me know if there is anything I can do to help you get ready for the children."

Minna stepped inside and said good night. She watched Robert make his way back to the schoolhouse. She shook her head. *Now that's dedication! Guess I don't have it so bad...*

Laguna
June 7, 1945

Dear Ernest Leigh,

I have no way of knowing when you will get this. There is no mail service here in Laguna. I will give my letters to my school board contact to mail in Albuquerque.

I hope they will come soon to give me some direction so I can get started with the lessons and get this summer over with!

I have met some of the children from the village now, so I am feeling a little better about things.

The folks at home have promised to send your letters to me as I know you probably can't write to all of us individually. I am anxious to hear how you are getting along. If you know how Frank is, I would appreciate you letting me in on it. I have not heard from him. Would you please tell him where I am and give him the Albuquerque address?

There is a very nice young missionary that shares the schoolhouse space with me. He says he will be praying for you. Surely this war will be over soon!

Take care. Your loving sister,
Minna

***

Mrs. Salita was enjoying herself immensely. Two of her friends had come to help get the school room ready for Minna's classes.

Robert felt obligated to pitch in and Minna came to help without being asked. *How wonderful!*

Mrs. Salita had heated a pan of water and given Minna the task of washing the grimy windows. Cold water would not have worked nearly so well to give Minna's face that rosy glow from heat and exertion. *Just lovely!* Minna's hair was tied up in a scarf, just like the other women. Little tendrils of hair had crept out, framing her face attractively.

Mrs. Salita hoped Robert had noticed and was appreciative of the effect. She had given him the job of plastering the cracks in the walls, placing him in close proximity to Minna. The old woman dusted all the meager furnishings and kept a close watch on how often Robert stole glances at her tenant. She strained to hear what they had to say.

"You will be surprised, Miss Cagle, at how beautiful these adobe houses can look, inside and out," Robert commented. Mrs. Salita groaned inwardly.

Eh Hiay! Reverend, ask her something personal!

"Yes, I am amazed that such material can be so attractive and comfortable." Minna said.

Mrs. Salita shook her head in frustration. *Now Robert, get to know about what she likes…*

"When we finish plastering, we will calcium wash the walls and it will be considerably more cheerful in here." Robert said.

What's wrong with you, Reverend? It was certainly clear to Mrs. Salita that Robert needed her help!

She said sweetly, "When we get done here, how about I pack a picnic lunch and you can show Miss Cagle that place you like so much up on the mesa?"

Robert frowned. "Oh, I'm sorry. I promised to take Albert and Leon out to their sheep camp when we are finished."

There was an uncomfortable silence. Albert was one of Mrs. Salita's ex-husbands.

"Hmmph." Mrs. Salita shrugged. She slapped the wooden chairs with her dust rag a little too exuberantly. The other women glanced at each other and stifled giggles. "So, that old *moohs-hash-cheh-dze-she* wants a ride again?" Mrs. Salita asked.

Robert scratched his chin. "*Hah*, yes, he might be an old tom cat like you say, but I have had occasion to be grateful for his help. I am happy to give him a ride if my automobile is agreeable to the task."

This won't do at all! Wish my ex would exit! Oh, I know....

"Let's all go up there! I bet Miss Cagle hasn't been up as far as Paraje mesas," Mrs. Salita said.

Robert turned to Minna, eyebrows raised. "It is some beautiful country up that way. Would you like to see?"

"*Hah!*" Minna made her first attempt at the Keresan language.

Mrs. Salita sighed in contentment. "All we like sheep have gone astray; we have turned every one to his own way; and the Lord hath laid on him the iniquity of us all..." she quoted. "The book of 'I-See-You' 53:6."

"I think you mean, ISAIAH." Robert said gently.

"That's right, 'I-Say-it." that's what I meant."

Minna thought her nose detected a sweet burning aroma, something like her father's pipe tobacco. The two women that had come to help were waving a burning bundle of herbs as they slowly walked around the school room. When Mrs. Salita saw her confused expression she said in a low voice, "They are saging. It clears the room of all negativity and I think it just smells better." She winked.

When the women had finished they joined Mrs. Salita, Minna and Robert in a circle and Robert was asked to say a blessing.

"Father, I thank you for this opportunity for a meeting place, both for our services in celebration of your blessings, and as a place of learning for Minna's students. Bless each person that comes through the door and help us to make this building an instrument of your peace. Amen."

Minna had bowed her head with the others but she peeked around the room as Robert prayed. She smiled at how much brighter and more cheerful the room looked. An instrument of peace…

"Amen!" She said heartily with the others.

THREE

Ia soo-nus shku-kuia gu-weshk koo-be-wa-tsi-shro.
(He maketh me to lie down in green pastures.)

Luckily, Robert's automobile was cooperative, so they all piled in "the toodlelooka" for the trip to sheep camp. Minna rode in back with Leon and Gloria. Robert's friend Albert rode up front with Mrs. Salita. She was not amused. Minna found Albert to be very quiet and hoped he was not feeling resentful of her presence at the last minute. She wondered if it was awkward for Mrs. Salita having to ride next to her ex-husband. Probably so, since her face was pinched up as if she were clenching her teeth.

Maybe that was why Albert was so quiet. He was a man that hid his age well, slight of build with laugh crinkles at his eyes. He appeared to be mostly sleeping in the front seat.

Gloria and Leon were talking a lot but it was at each other and in Keresan. It sounded like the normal bickering that married people do. Minna could almost imagine what they were saying.

"It was Wednesday, last."

"No, it was Thursday."

"What do you mean Thursday, you know it was Wednesday."

"I am telling you it was Thursday. I was there."

"Well, if you were there, then it wasn't Thursday!"

Law Me!

Albert opened his eyes and cleared his throat noisily. "So there is that commandment in the Jesus book about honor your father and mother, Robert. Is there one about husbands and wives?"

"Yes," Robert was grinning. "Thou shall not kill…"

24

They certainly did see some beautiful country. Minna never knew there were rock formations with so many pretty colors. The mountains were different from the mostly blues and greens in the Appalachians back east. *Just breathtaking!* The highest mountain in the distance was Mt. Taylor she was told, also known to the Indians as Turquoise Mountain. It did seem, from this distance, to have a bluish hue.

If Minna thought the road was bumpy before, she was quickly re-educated. She was not sure if this bone jarring last leg of the journey could even be considered a road. Empty desert gave way to brushy plants and larger spiky leaved bushes.

"Are those cactus?" Minna asked.

"No, yucca plants and Joshua trees," Gloria provided. "I think they look like little Kokopellis."

"Pardon?"

"Kokopelli. It's a figure the ancients carved on rocks. It looks like a bent over little man wearing a war bonnet."

Minna peered out the car window.

"Yes, I see that."

They had entered a canyon between two towering mesas. There sheltered in the long shadows, was a campfire near a simple wooden shack. Several men crouched over a stew pot. They stood up one by one as the toodlelooka came to a halt.

Many "*Ga-wa-tses*" and introductions later, they all had a bite to eat in the peaceful shade of late afternoon. Minna was fascinated to finally see green grass in New Mexico. Enjoying that grass was a rolling, bleating mass of sheep. The way they ran together in every direction made them look like a great white woolen blanket being shaken out over the canyon. She could understand why they were kept here. There was nowhere for them to escape. With high rock walls in three directions, and shepherds in the fourth to prevent it. Yet, as she looked out over the flock it appeared a few were attempting it anyway. There were sheep standing in the natural indentations in the rock wall, high over the others.

Minna wound her way through the flock to get a closer look and was drawn to the sight of one young lamb so high up above the others, she couldn't determine how it got up nor how it would get back down.

Gloria had followed her and pushed away the more curious of the sheep surrounding them. She swatted at the ones nibbling at their clothes.

"They sometimes get up there too far," Gloria said. "Then once they are trapped, one of us has to climb up there and bring them back."

Minna watched the lamb a little while longer. She felt a little like the lost lamb herself. Who would rescue her from New Mexico? Frank?

Gloria looked upward, "It's a good omen," she said. Minna looked up where Gloria was watching a bird with a huge wingspan soaring above them.

"Eagle." Gloria said. "They are very powerful and fly the highest. The people believe they carry their prayers up to heaven."

Minna could hear its high pitched shrill call. What a wonderful view of the canyon it must have!

***

Back at the camp Mrs. Salita sat with the men around the campfire in total frustration. Why didn't Robert follow Minna when she wandered off? Instead, he was sitting here jawing with these men! What a waste of time!

"Is there good fishing up here, Albert?" Robert asked.

"*Hah.* Good for spit fishing."

"Spit fishing?"

"*Hah.* I go out in a boat and throw in a chaw of tobacco. When the fish comes up to spit, I hit him with the oar!"

Everyone chuckled appreciatively.

Everyone, except Mrs. Salita.

"Well, I don't know," Robert said. "The last time I tried fishing from a boat, I fished all day with nary a bite. I had just given up and was putting my gear away, ready to come back to shore, when an enormous trout broke the water and landed right in my boat!"

26

"What'd you do?" Leon asked.

"I threw him back in! If he ain't gonna bite, he ain't gonna ride!"

Mrs. Salita threw her hands up in exasperation and stomped off to join Minna and Gloria. They were both watching the enormous bird until it flew out of sight. Mrs. Salita reached down to pick up a couple of smooth stones in their path.

"Polishing stones." She showed them to Minna.

"Polishing stones?"

"*Hah.* We don't glaze our pots, we rub them with these and that makes them shine."

Minna remembered the beautiful pottery Gloria and Mrs. Salita had taken to Santa Fe. How she wished she could afford to buy them for her family back home!

When they turned back toward the clump of men around the campfire, Robert was waving them in.

"We'd better start back," Mrs. Salita said. "It will be dark soon."

They left Albert and Leon there at the camp and Robert, Gloria, Mrs. Salita and Minna approached the toodelooka.

"How did you like sheep camp?" Robert asked Minna.

"Inspirational!" she replied.

"Disappointing," Mrs. Salita muttered under her breath. *Still, there is the ride back...* "You sit up front with Robert," she said to Minna. "Gloria and I will sit in the back."

After nearly a half an hour of silence Mrs. Salita cleared her throat.

"Would you like to hear a pueblo story about the Eagle?"

"Yes!" Robert and Minna said together.

"Once there was a boy that had an eagle as a pet. When the boy went hunting for food to bring his family he always brought something for the eagle as well. But he had to go farther and farther away to find good hunting so one day he tied his eagle to the roof by its leg and he asked his sister to take care of the eagle while he was away.

The girl was jealous of the eagle. She didn't understand why the boy would give it the best food instead of giving the best to his family. She gave the eagle only scraps to eat.

27

When the boy got back he could see his sister had given the eagle only scraps because the eagle had not touched them.

'Friend eagle, why have you not eaten?' asked the boy.

'Because I am not wanted here. Untie my leg so I can fly back home to my eagle family.'

'But I want you to stay with me,' said the boy.

'Your sister does not want me. Untie my leg and I will take you with me to where the eagles live.'

The boy had always wondered what it would be like to fly like an eagle so he untied the eagle's leg and climbed on the eagle's back.

They flew higher and higher and the boy became afraid so the eagle told him to close his eyes. At last they came to the place where the eagles lived.

When the boy opened his eyes there were eagles everywhere. They came right up to him and he was not afraid of them and they were not afraid of him. The boy stayed with the eagles for a long time because he was so happy with them. But one day his pet eagle came to him and said, 'It is time for you to go home. Your family needs you.' So the eagles gave the boy many presents. The chief of the eagles told the boy, 'We are just like you. We do not like to be tied up by our legs. Don't do that anymore to any eagle. Let the eagles live here where we belong.'

The boy climbed on the eagle's back and closed his eyes. The eagle flew to the village and set him down. The boy gave the presents the eagles had given him to his family and he told the people of his village what the eagle chief had told him. 'The eagles are just the same as us,' he said. 'They do not like to be tied up.'

So to this day. Eagles are not kept as pets as they used to be.

***

That night Minna thought she was having a good dream. There was Frank! He looked so handsome in his uniform. She ran to him and threw her arms around his neck. But in her dream Frank gently pushed her arms away.

"Frank, what's wrong?" Minna said in disappointment.

"We are just like the eagles, Minna." Frank said. "We do not like to be tied up."

Sunday, June 10, 1945

Minna sat at the back of the school room and observed the service Robert was conducting. He certainly was like no other preacher she had ever heard. He used an interpreter as he quietly put his thoughts across to the small crowd assembled there. Minna noted that in addition to the interpreter he frequently used phrases in the Keresan language himself. She, therefore, had a little trouble following all of it.

She realized she probably should have moved to the front of the room in order to hear better, but she didn't want to be "on display."

The children had other ideas as they openly stared at her, wide eyed.

They must be as terrified of me as I am of them!

She tried smiling encouragingly to the little face straining to look at her. The child ducked down abruptly in his seat and hid his eyes.

Law me! She touched the angel brooch on her hat. It was still secure but oh, she wished now she had not worn it! Gazing out over the small gathering she noted no one else was wearing a hat. She felt she stuck out like a sore thumb. A sore thumb wearing a hat!

Robert continued with his scripture reference, "How think ye? If a man have an hundred sheep, and one of them be gone astray, doth he not leave the ninety and nine, and go into the mountains, and seek that which is gone astray?"

Now that she had been to sheep camp, Minna thought she knew how Robert came to choose this scripture for today's sermon. She tried to concentrate but her thoughts kept jumping back to Frank. Was he lost or captured? She had to find out! *Why hasn't he tried to contact me?*

After the service Robert introduced Minna to his interpreter, Mrs. Day. She was a very pleasant woman with soft gray hair and a round flat face.

"This is my Keresan teacher," Robert said. "She has been helping me translate some of the hymns in the hymn book into the Keresan language. I read a line in English and she says it back in Keresan, then I can write it phonetically in the hymn book."

Minna grew excited. That could be a way of helping the children too, she thought.

"Mrs. Day, could you help me with something similar, using the readers I brought with me from home?" Minna asked.

"Of course! I would be happy to help."

Mrs. Salita suddenly appeared at Robert's side. "Mrs. Day, Robert, why don't you both come have a meal with us?"

"Certainly!" Robert seemed eager to do so. Minna guessed it must get pretty old cooking over a kerosene lamp.

Mrs. Salita had baked bread the day before in the adobe oven outside her house. It was a round igloo-like structure that reminded Minna of a dog house. She had watched Mrs. Salita prepare a hot fire inside the oven, letting the wood burn completely up. Then she swept out the ashes and placed the round loaves of dough inside and closed the hole. The bread was delicious, even if it had come from a dog house!

"If I keep eating like this, I will be able to roll myself back home at summer's end, just like a big ol' ball." Minna said.

"My doctor tried to put me on a diet once," Robert said straight faced. "He told me if anything tastes good in my mouth, I should spit it out!"

Mrs. Salita and Mrs. Day tittered.

Minna asked Robert, "Is that true?"

"Not quite hardly, but 'most pert' nearly."

Mrs. Day agreed to help Robert and Minna with a language lesson after they had eaten. Robert fetched his hymnbook and Minna chose one of the first grade readers she had brought from home. They would each read a line from their books and Mrs. Day repeated it back to them in Keresan. Then they wrote it phonetically in their books and attempted to read it back to Mrs. Day.

Robert's hymn of choice was "What A Friend We Have In Jesus." Minna's story was about a little boy and his new wagon.

"See my new wagon." Minna read.

"*Pookch na-tze gar-redth sa-a-she.*" Mrs. Day said back. Minna wrote it in her book.

"What a Friend we have in Jesus," Robert read.

"*He-su Chre-sto Sa-u-ke-nyi,*" Mrs. Day said back. Robert wrote it in his hymnal.

It was Minna's turn. "I will let you ride in my wagon."

"*Uts hoh-dyu shrup-oo-nia-e.*" Mrs. Day said.

They heard a voice calling for Mrs. Salita at her front door.

"All our sins and griefs to bear," Robert said.

"*Sau-ke-tshe kiat-su-wa-Nye.*"

"Grandmother said, 'I'm too big'," Minna read.

"*Ga ba-ba dyu-na-da, ma-me sech.*"

"*Ma-me sech?*" Minna repeated, turning her good ear to Mrs. Day.

Just as she did that, Mrs. Salita and her neighbor, Rose came into the room. Rose was a very large woman!

"*Hah,*" said Rose. "*Ma-me sech!*"

Minna was embarrassed most to death, but the neighbor took it in good humor and they all laughed about it.

Minna tugged on her good ear. *Law me! Now I've insulted the neighbor!*

***

The next morning Robert woke to the sound of drums. They must be quite near as he felt them reverberate through his chest as he lay in his iron bed. *Uh, oh! Better get up!*

He hastened to dress and spruce up the school room. He knew from experience that the drums meant a council meeting would be held at the schoolhouse.

After a quick breakfast of fruit and vanilla wafers, he began lining up folding chairs in hopes that the council would approve of his willingness to relinquish the schoolroom to their meeting.

It always made him a little nervous when such meetings occurred. He knew there were some on the council that simply didn't want him there. Thankfully so far, they had been in the minority and their grumblings had been of no consequence.

The first to arrive was the governor of the reservation.

"*Ga-wa-tse!*" Robert greeted him, holding the door wide.

"*Ga-wa-tse*, Robert!" The man entered smiling broadly. He was holding a large box of crackers. "These are for you, I hear you like them."

This was a good sign, Robert realized. He had been using saltine crackers when they had communion in his services.

"So how is your pretty little school teacher working out?" The governor teased.

Robert found himself blushing. "Why, I can hardly claim her as my own my friend, but she is an attractive young lady. I'm sure the children will love her."

"That is the council's wish. We would like for the two of you to attend our banquet this afternoon after the council meeting."

"I would be honored and I will tell Miss Cagle to come."

The council members arrived and filed into the schoolroom. Robert decided to make himself scarce.

***

Minna didn't know how Mrs. Salita had managed to seat her next to the governor of Laguna reservation at the council banquet, but there she was! What an honor to be seated with the governor at the end of the table on her right and the secretary of the Indian council to her left. *Now I really have something to write home about!*

The secretary was a neat young man. He wore a western shirt buttoned all the way up and had short slicked back hair. The governor was older, with graying hair and wrinkled face. He also wore a western shirt with a bolo tie.

Robert sat across from her and the rest of the council filled the other seats at the table.

The food was amazing! Minna felt like she had sampled every kind of chili ever invented. She wondered how anything that hurt that much could taste so good! Still, the chili peppers were making her warmer and warmer and she was sure her face was getting red. She kept refilling her water glass.

"Here." Robert offered her some crusty bread. "I have learned it softens the peppers more than water." He reached for more bread and offered the plate to Minna. "When I first arrived I was so anxious to be polite at these banquets. If someone asked me if I liked the peppers, I always said '*hah!*' But I soon learned if I did that they understood me to mean I wanted more and would oblige by making my plate hotter and hotter! My face was as red as yours on more than one occasion."

"What did you do then?" Minna wanted to know.

"If anyone asks if you like it and you don't want any more, say, 'I enjoyed it thank you, but I don't need any more yet.'"

The women at the next table found Minna amusing. She noticed how they were giggling and talking to one another in their language while stealing glances at her. Finally, she got bold enough to ask Robert what was so funny.

"They are saying you eat like a rabbit," he said, demonstrating with a wiggling nose. He listened further with his head tilted. "Oh." Robert suppressed a giggle of his own.

"What, Robert? What are they saying?" Minna asked nervously.

"Miss Cagle, please don't be offended. It is an honor to be given an Indian name…"

"An Indian name? What name?"

"*Tskoo-nuts dru-sish dze-she-tshe dyety.*" The governor chimed in. "It means, 'Little rabbit wiggle nose'."

Suddenly the entire table got very quiet. Minna squirmed in her seat. She sensed the moment was important somehow and she chose her words carefully.

"Well, that is better, I suppose, than something like, 'Eats like a horse' which is what I feel like I'm doing."

The table exploded in laughter and everyone began talking at once.

Robert beamed with pride.

"What is your Indian name, Robert?" Minna asked him.

He put his fork down and cleared his throat. "*Kenuty*," he said.

"Which means?"

"Green corn."

"Green horn?" It was hard for Minna to hear with so many voices speaking all at once.

"Green corn. I think it is because my hair is the color of corn tassel when the ears are first growing and considered green."

"I like green horn better." The governor said.

After Minna had eaten all that she could hold and then some, the school board official from Albuquerque finally made an appearance at the schoolroom. Minna excused herself from the few council members that were left at the banquet and made her way to the schoolhouse.

Esmae Pynchon made a striking picture. She was dressed in an expensive beige, tone on tone plaid suit. Her platinum blond hair was piled high in an extreme up-do. It brought to Minna's mind the soft serve ice cream cone she had experienced in Chicago. There was an enormous fabric flower pinned to Miss Pynchon's shoulder. *Law me, it's a dress wearing a lady!*

Minna couldn't help but feel very nervous around Miss Pynchon, but she tried not to let it show. They were observing the classroom and Miss Pynchon did not look pleased!

"I suppose this is all there is, Miranda. Education does not depend on the sophistication of the classroom facilities."

"Minna. It's Minna." To her embarrassment Minna burped loudly. She clutched her hand over her mouth. "Please excuse me. I'm afraid I ate entirely too much at the banquet." She pointed to the folding chairs. "I was hoping for desks at least."

"Well, clearly there aren't any desks yet. You will have to be creative and make do with these." She indicated the folding chairs. "Just focus on the students and their abilities. What is that odor?" Miss Pynchon said, sniffing the air.

Robert came around his privacy curtain. "I'm sorry. I'm *afred* it is the remains of my lunch. We had so much food at the banquet, I thought I would save some of it for my supper tonight."

Minna noticed that Miss Pynchon's demeanor changed immediately. "Who are you?" Miss Pynchon tilted her head beguilingly.

"I'm Robert Carlisle." He offered his hand. "I share the space with Miss Cagle but I will try my best to stay out of the way."

"Oh, yes. Seems I've heard of you. I didn't realize you were so…young Mr. Carlisle." Miss Pynchon pulled her shoulders back. With a straight back and the up-do she was taller than Robert. "I am Esmae Pynchon, Mr. Carlisle. I will be dropping in from time to time to observe Mildred here."

"It's Minna," Minna corrected her again.

"Well, welcome Miss Pynchon. Would you ladies care for some chili and crackers?"

Minna and Miss Pynchon glanced at each other. There was an uncomfortable silence.

"No, thank you," Miss Pynchon said.

"No, thank you. I've done enough damage already." Minna held back another burp.

"It's too bad you weren't here for the council banquet, Miss Pynchon, but there is probably plenty of food left if you haven't eaten," Robert said.

Miss Pynchon wrinkled her nose. "I am not fond of native foods, Mr. Carlisle."

Minna was not sure what to make of Miss Pynchon. She seemed professional and organized but there was something decidedly sour about her. This was a person with a high opinion of herself. Still, she had at least brought Minna's mail and ration books from Albuquerque, so she was grateful to see her. There was no letter from Ernest Leigh and still no word from Frank. There was a letter from her mother and one from her little sister. Minna put them away for later so that she could read them in private.

Minna spent the rest of the day showing Miss Pynchon the books she had brought and discussing with her how she planned to help the children learn English as she had been contracted to do. Miss Pynchon was unimpressed with the books. "You don't have to teach them to read you know. Just teach them the rudimentary elements of the English language. You know, enough to get by when their formal education starts in the fall."

"I thought perhaps the pictures would help with that."

"Yes, well. I suppose visual aids are what they are stressing in teacher training these days."

Minna had no reply. It was evident what Miss Pynchon thought of her qualifications. *More reason to feel nervous!*

Miss Pynchon gave one final look at the classroom before her departure. "You may start lessons any time the local council gives permission, Margaret."

"Minna." She tried not to let her irritation show.

Minna had mixed feelings. She was anxious to get started, yet at the same time, terrified to do just that. She consoled herself thinking how wonderful it would be when the war was over and Ernest Leigh and Frank came home! Maybe by then she would have fulfilled her obligations in New Mexico and could meet Frank with her head held high and no more debt to her name! Then what would prevent them from a future together? None of this would matter then. Still, what a relief to see Miss Pynchon go!

Minna stood in the doorway and watched Miss Pynchon's automobile pull away from the schoolhouse.

Whew! Hope she didn't notice how scared I was!

Minna patted the two letters in her pocket. She eagerly walked across the dusty road to Mrs. Salita's house. It was good to hear from home so soon after arriving in Laguna.

Minna moved to the window in her room, where the light was better and pulled her sister's letter out of her pocket. Turning it over in the light, she noticed the post mark was the day she had left home and begun her journey out west. She tore it open. She smiled as she read;

Sweetwater,
June 1

Dear MinnieBee,

You just left this morning and I already miss you! Just so you know, Ma'un is making me do your chores as well as mine! I think she is being mean to me because she is worried about you. So write as soon as you get a chance and let her know you are okay!

Seems to me the twins just play all the time and I am the one scrubbing dishes and sweeping floors.

Oh, well, I am going on a picnic with my friends next Saturday. Ma'un says she will show me how to make potato salad like she does.

Guess this is all I know for now. Are there any cute boys in New Mexico?

Write us soon!
Sissy

Minna smiled as she stuffed the letter back in the envelope and placed it on top of the dresser.

She opened the letter from her mother. It was postmarked the day after Sissy's.

As Minna read her smile faded to a face full of worry lines.

Sweetwater,
June 2

Dear Minerva,

I am sorry to bring you bad news so soon after you left. I don't know when you will receive this, but you need to know.

We have received a telegram informing us that your brother, Ernest Leigh, has been seriously wounded.

We don't have any details as to how bad or when or where but they say he is on a hospital ship and as soon as he is well enough they will send him home.

We hope this means they expect him to recover.

Sissy and the twins are taking this hard but your Pa and me are thinking it is almost a blessing in that now we will have him home and not at war.

Hope you have arrived safely,
Your Ma

Minna gulped back tears. *Oh, Ernest Leigh! I was afraid of this. Oh, please be all right! How silly of me to be afraid of teaching school children when you have had to face so much more! If only prayers would help...*

FOUR

Ke shku-i-oots ia-e tsits beshch tse-e-shro.
(He leadeth me beside the still waters.)

What an amazing woman!

Robert admired Minna's antics with the children. She was acting out an amusing story with many gestures and facial expressions.

How clever of her to use the two Keresan words she knew, *"Ga-wa-tse"* and *"Dyety"*, to make up a story about a little rabbit making new friends. It helped the children learn, "hello, my name is…" in English. The twenty or so children were warming up to her and seemed to be enjoying her story whether they understood much of it or not.

Robert had intended to spend the day seeking new spark plugs for the toodlelooka, but he just couldn't seem to tear himself away from Minna and her new class.

He hoped she hadn't noticed how rattled he had felt Sunday at services. He just couldn't seem to concentrate on his sermon! Maybe he had been showing off a little using so many Keresan phrases. *What is wrong with me?*

Best not to get too enamored of this one, pretty as she is. She is only contracted for the summer and who knows, come autumn, if I will ever see her again? Yes, maybe I had better go see about the car.

Laguna, New Mexico
June 12, 1945

Hey Sam!

'Bout time you heard from your big brother, eh? So how are you getting along? Me, heap fine!

38

I am so glad to hear you will be stationed at Dalhart, Texas. It is not so far from me. I could come visit when you get there. Let me know.

Dave tells me you are getting serious with this girl, Louise. I am thrilled plumb silly to hear it! Hope you will find the time to write to me at the Albuquerque address some of these days.

Your brother,
Robert

Robert smiled at the photograph his brother had sent him. It was Sam, in uniform, sitting at a restaurant table with his arm around his girl. Robert was happy to think that after the horrors of war, Sam could come home to start a life with a loving wife at his side. It was an appealing thought.

Father forgive me, I think I feel a little sibling rivalry and jealousy here.

***

Minna felt like her job was well underway.

It was a challenge daily to keep the children engaged and attentive. A regular gang of older boys played various mischievous pranks outside while she was trying to have lessons. Some days she had to give up and send the students home, the outside disturbance was so bad.

When Robert was around, all he had to do was open the door and the boys would scatter. Today, however, he was away visiting some of the sick folk in his congregation, so Minna had the school room to herself.

When the usual shenanigans started outside, she gritted her teeth in determination. Nothing or no one was going to keep her from fulfilling her summer contract! She was ready for them this time!

She excused herself politely from the children, grabbed the reader she had been using with Mrs. Day's help, and flipped to the page she had dog-eared.

Opening the door wide, she yelled with the full capacity of her lung power, *"Ba-me gu-nu-she-u dye-eh gu-i-a!"* (Do stop that noise*!)* *"Wia-she setw shia-yu-u-i-shi-yu-gia!"* (You have played enough tricks today!)

For once the boys did not scatter but stood in gaping mouth wonderment at this unexpected outburst.

Minna harrumphed, smoothed her skirt and turned back to the students inside.

The children broke into thunderous applause.

Minna had her back turned to the door when Robert slipped into the schoolhouse with a bag of groceries. He put them away quietly but kept peeping around his privacy curtain. Although he seemed anxious not to disturb the class, it was clear he was fidgeting about something.

Minna seemed unaware of his agitation, but the children noticed.

One child tried to whisper in her ear. Minna turned to the little girl.

"I'm sorry honey, I am deaf in my left ear. What were you trying to tell me?"

The child pursed her lips and jerked her head toward Robert's end of the room.

Robert continued his fidgeting.

Law me! Does he think he needs my permission to visit the privy?

Minna hurried her lesson along. She wanted to know what had Robert's skivvies tied in a knot.

When the last student had left the building she asked him, her voice burning with curiosity, "Robert, what is it?"

"Miss Cagle, I have just been to the store here on the reservation and you know they have a radio there..."

"Yes..."

"I heard that there has been a heavy gun battle on Okinawa and many suicides among the Japanese forces. Our boys have been under heavy fire. Do you think your brother could be involved in that?"

Minna bit her lip.

"I haven't had the chance to tell you Robert, my brother has already been seriously hurt and is on a hospital ship somewhere in the Pacific. He could have very well been involved in the fighting there in Japan. But oh Robert, this could be good news, right? If we can defeat the Japanese on their own territory won't the war be over soon?"

"I pray that is true," he said sincerely. "And most certainly I will continue to keep your brother in my prayers."

**

That night Minna tossed and turned in her bed, unable to sleep. Dare she offer up a prayer on her brother and Frank's behalf?

So risky!

If either one of them didn't make it home she didn't know if she could forgive God for that answer!

And yet, what else could she do? She felt so helpless against this war! How could her loved ones go so willingly?

They believed they would be all right. Was it because of their own prayers?

Minna longed to talk to Robert about it but she was afraid to let him know how she felt. She was sure he would be disappointed in her for thinking such things.

Minna finally gave up on trying to sleep. She slipped out of her bed and padded across the floor to the kerosene lamp on the little table by the window. After she had lit the lamp she took her writing materials out and sat down to write by the shadowy light cast by the lamp.

Dear Frank,

I am sending this to the last address I have for you and I hope it gets to the right place.

I hope you are doing all right. I'm sure you must know at least a little news about Ernest Leigh's situation. Please if you can, write and tell me how you are. I am so very worried about both of you!

I am doing the best I can in this summer job. Most of the time I hardly know what I'm doing. What really keeps me going is believing this war will soon be over and we can be safely together again. I hope you feel the same. Please write.

> *With love,*
> *Minna*

The next morning Minna came to the school room feeling bleary eyed and depressed.

When thoughts of Ernest Leigh and Frank nagged at her, she pushed them aside and concentrated on the job at hand.

One of the children noticed her subdued mood and approached her shyly. When Minna looked up the little girl put her hand gently on top of Minna's.

"Shroh sawakdyeu shuiyunu," the child said softly.

"I'm sorry, honey. I don't understand." Minna said.

The little girl placed a rag doll in Minna's hand.

Minna looked at the other children questioningly.

"She wants to give you her doll, Miss Minna," one of the children offered.

Should she take it? Minna's heart melted with appreciation that the child wanted her to feel better.

I'll take it for now and return it to her later. Minna smiled at the little girl warmly.

"Da-wa-eh," she whispered.

***

That afternoon Minna had a mind to wash clothes but the wind was blowing so hard, she knew they would not have stayed on the line. Even if they did, they would have been full of sand.

Mrs. Salita was kind enough to let her hang her wet clothes up in the house. That is what they were doing when they heard the automobile horn blowing in the village.

"Here comes Robert in the toodlelooka," Mrs. Salita noted.

Minna peered out the window. Robert's automobile was coming around the school building, filled to distraction with shouting children. One of them was steering! Minna smiled at the sight. Robert and two other men were pushing. The children scrambled out. The men lifted the hood of the automobile and leaned over the engine. Minna could not hear the conversation but it was clear Robert was having car trouble again.

After awhile, Robert came to the house with a box of things for Mrs. Salita. He placed it on the kitchen table after winding through a gauntlet of Minna's wet garments.

"To market to market to look for a roast..." he said cheerfully. "Home again, home again, tuna on toast."

Mrs. Salita was beaming as she unloaded the box.

"*Da-wa-eh! Da-wa-eh!* Reverend you must eat with us!"

"*Eh-hiay, Naya. Hah, da-wa-eh.*"

They all sat down amongst the laundry to a sumptuous feast of corn, tamales, and pinto beans.

"We have decided the toodlelooka needs a replacement coil and some of the men from the village think they know where to find one. If we can get my automobile running again, I will go out to sheep camp to pick up Albert and Leon."

Mrs. Salita made a point of loudly clearing her throat, "Gloria is hoping to go with you to pick up Leon and Albert. How about you go with them too, *Dyety*?"

Minna had enjoyed the trip to the Paraje mesas the week before, so she agreed to go.

Mrs. Salita waved out the window as Robert, Gloria, and Minna pulled away from the school building in the toodlelooka. Children ran alongside the automobile to the edge of the village, calling to Robert and "Miss Minna". When they progressed about a mile outside Laguna, Robert grabbed the steering wheel with his full weight. He was losing control of the toodlelooka! Startled, Minna's hands flew to her face. Robert was finally able to pull over to the side of the road. They had a flat tire!

Robert groaned as he climbed out of the driver's seat and stood beside the toodlelooka scratching his head.

"This is going to set back our trip considerably, I'm *afred*."
He leaned into the open window on Minna's side of the toodlelooka.
"I don't know how long this will take to change the tire. Maybe
you and Gloria should hike back to Laguna. It's not far if you go
as the crow flies over the rise there."

Robert assured them there was nothing they could do to
help so Minna and Gloria reluctantly left him there.

The route they took was a path across the sandy terrain, the
shortest way. Minna didn't realize it would involve a hazardous
crossing by a bridge made for pedestrians. It wasn't much more
than a log laid across a chasm which seemed to her awesomely
deep and broad. At least there was a handrail!

Gloria went first as quick and surefooted as a mountain
goat.

It was only by her encouragement and coaxing that Minna
was able to slowly follow, holding on to the hand rail for dear
life.

Robert would be proud of me, she thought, due to the
amount of praying she was doing just to get across. Somehow she
managed it and they continued on toward the village. Just as the
adobe houses of the village loomed ahead, about a half dozen boys
from the village caught up with them. Minna wondered if they
were some of the ones that had been disturbing her class.

"*Ga-wa-tse*," Gloria and Minna both said. Minna was very
glad to have Gloria with her to translate if needed.

One of the boys said something to Gloria and she told
Minna, "He wants to know if you get scared walking alone?"

Minna considered whether or not he was making some
kind of threat.

"Tell him no," she said. "I don't feel like I'm alone. Tell
him I doubt if anything could be more scary than that bridge back
there."

Gloria translated and they all seemed to think her reply
very funny.

One of the boys sniggered with his hand over his mouth
then said in English, "Wouldn't you get scared, if an elephant was
chasing you?"

Minna stopped to remove a pebble from her shoe. "Well, I might if that happened. But I don't think there are any elephants in New Mexico."

"How about coyotes?"

"I have never seen one," Minna said. "Although maybe I have heard them some in the morning."

She had no sooner said this than they began talking to one another in Keresan and the next thing she knew they were yipping and howling and chasing each other around like a pack of coyotes.

Gloria picked up a stick and let forth a barrage of angry words in Keresan. Minna stopped in her tracks, wide eyed.

"Are you all right?" Gloria asked her.

Minna nodded her head and walked forward again.

They made it back to the village in spite of the commotion, unharmed, only shaken a bit. Gloria kept up a steady stream of rapid Keresan and continued it to her mother once they arrived.

Mrs. Salita kept saying "*Eh-hiay, eh-hiay!*"

***

Sunday, June 17, 1945

Robert cleared his throat.

"If I seem a little hoarse this morning it is because I think I somehow managed to catch a cold and my throat is full of bumblebees." The congregation tittered appreciatively.

As Robert began his sermon he noticed some boys filing into the back of the room. Right behind them came Mrs. Salita with a grim face full of determination.

Robert laid his notes aside and continued, "I see we have some young people visiting with us today. Welcome! I feel compelled to share a story with you from my youth. Perhaps you will find it meaningful.

"When we were youngsters, my older brother Dave seemed to delight in teasing me mercilessly.

"We all loved the day in springtime when we were allowed to go barefoot outdoors. At last Daddy had decided the ground was warm enough and we could go barefoot if we wanted to.

"So the first day I was walking home on the wagon road with Dave, and I was discovering the sharp cornered little gravel were hurting my bare feet, a turn of events that neither I nor this taunting brother of mine could ignore.

"I couldn't fight him of course, and I knew it, but I could throw a rock! I picked up a pebble about the size of a robin's egg and let it fly, intending to sting him a little where his clothes protected his body. But, oops!

"My aim was far from perfect, and the pebble hit him in the forehead, causing a knot to swell forth, grim evidence of my crime. Dave didn't say anything, but gave a little squeak, and for the only time I remember, I had brought tears to his eyes.

"My mother was in the hospital at the time and my Aunt Lizzie was appalled when she heard what I had done. She decided the best thing for me to do would be to go down to the field where Daddy was plowing and confess to him my guilt and my shame.

"I had to follow a while in the furrow behind Daddy before I could muster the courage to speak.

'Daddy, I hit Dave with a rock.'

'What?'

'I hit Dave with a rock.'

'Did you hurt him?'

'I guess so.'

'Why did you do such a thing?'

'I was mad at him.'

'What were you mad about?'

'He was teasing me.'

'What was he teasing you about?'

"At this point I was embarrassed by a lapse in my memory. All I could say was, 'I don't remember.'

'I will have to punish you,' said Daddy. 'You go to the edge of the woods and get me a switch, while I unhitch the horses and put them in the stable.'

"I thought of running away, but instinctively knew that I couldn't get very far. I arrived with the switch I had carefully selected. I must admit it was a rather puny one.

'That's no switch for whipping a boy,' he exclaimed.

46

"Somehow I managed to muster enough courage and voice to feebly ask, 'shall I go and get another one?'

'No, son. I've decided that since you came and told me what you have done, I won't whip you, but don't ever do such a thing again.'

"I was totally unprepared for this welcome surprise. I had resolved to take my whipping without a whimper, but now I simply could not hold back my tears and my wailing. I guess Daddy knew me better than I knew myself and he taught me three important lessons that day.

"Lesson #1: When we send a missile in anger, does it ever have the effect we intended?

"Lesson #2: Our Father in Heaven, the same as our earthly father, is greatly disappointed when we do things that hurt others, yet He still loves us and only wants the assurance that we are trying to please Him and get along with each other.

"Lesson #3: Our one real hope of mercy and pardon is to come and honestly confess our faults and ask His forgiveness. It may bring agonizing tears, but also relief and peace. I am sure my Daddy was familiar with the comforting message of 1 John 1:9. 'If we confess our sins, He is faithful and just to forgive us our sins, and to cleanse us from all unrighteousness."

After the service was over Mrs. Salita marched the boys over to Robert.

"*Shro-o,* let's go." She all but pushed them up the aisle. "This is Sandy, Amos, Carlos and George," she said. "They have something to say to you."

Robert tilted his head and lifted an eyebrow, his expression friendly.

"Go ahead." Mrs. Salita nudged the boy closest to her. He mumbled something and she elbowed him.

"S-s-s-sorry," he said, meekly.

"Yes, yes," Mrs. Salita prompted, "tell him sorry for what."

"F-for throwing dirt clods at the building."

"I see." Robert looked appropriately serious. "Do you have something against me, George? Or something against Miss Cagle?"

"It was because our parents say there shouldn't be church here." The second boy blurted.

"Why, Carlos?"

"They say we should only have church up the hill at the mission and school there too, with the nuns!"

"So you think they want you to throw dirt at us?" Robert asked gently.

'N-n-no." Carlos hung his head.

"I guess that was our idea." Amos offered. "We're sorry though. I like it when you tell stories in the village…and that chicken song." Amos was grinning.

Mrs. Salita motioned for Minna to join them. "You need to say this to *Dyety* too."

Minna came over to join the little group. "Sorry," three of the boys said together. Everyone looked expectantly at the fourth boy, Sandy.

"Well," Mrs. Salita said.

Sandy grimaced, then said explosively, "I wasn't down here!"

"You were there last night with the coyote boys weren't you?" Mrs. Salita wasn't going to let any of them off the hook.

"We were just fun'in'."

***

Minna had to smile, thinking of her brother when he was the age of these boys. That was exactly what he would have said! Her thoughts twirled back to their childhood where she recalled Ernest Leigh had a talent for making her take the blame for his shenanigans.

When they were teenagers Ernest Leigh had been asked to drive the school bus to where they attended high school in Niota, Tennessee.

It was a long way and a weary journey on the crowded bus so the passengers tried to find ways to amuse themselves along the way.

One of the fun things Minna recalled was to make up ridiculous rhymes for the saying, "Hail, hail, the gang's all here." It was so much fun, in fact, that she and Ernest Leigh continued the game at home at the supper table.

"Hail, hail, my wife's in jail."

"Hail, hail, we weep and wail."

"Hail, hail, fill up the pail."

"Hail, hail, my ship will sail."

Ernest Leigh had accidentally stepped on the dog's tail that was laying under the supper table and he came up with, "Hail, hail, get off my tail!"

Minna made the mistake of repeating it on the school bus the next day. She found to her surprise, that she was summoned to the principal's office. One of the passengers on the bus had "tattled" on her, saying she had been singing obscene songs on the bus!

Ernest Leigh was not implicated because he was the bus driver and above such things!

Where is he now, she wondered? Will he recover? Has Frank been wounded as well? Or even killed?

***

"I am proud of you boys," she heard Robert say. "I hope your parents will grow to understand our purpose here and allow us to be friends."

Satisfied, Mrs. Salita dismissed the boys. "All right then. You can go home now." She took Robert aside. "Robert, I want you to come over for lunch. I am going to cure your cold with my 'sinus restorative' soup!"

Whew! She wasn't kidding! Robert's face kept getting redder with every bite. It seemed to delight Mrs. Salita who kept encouraging him to have more.

They discussed the latest turn of events in hushed tones.

"I think they were just showing off, like boys that age do..." Minna was thinking of Ernest Leigh. Her brother had teased her enormously when they were children. Still did, on some occasions.

49

"Don't let them get away with this that easy! It is considered a deadly sin to be rude to visitors on the reservation. Those boys knew better! They were acting like they don't have relatives." Mrs. Salita put her coffee cup down with a thud, spilling some on the table cloth. "We did get some useful information from them though. I might have guessed some of the ones on the council were grumbling about using the schoolhouse. They never want anything to change."

"They have a right to their own opinions." Robert croaked through his sore throat. "Still, it is disconcerting that the boys wanted to pull enough pranks to make us want to leave…"

"I don't think they want us to leave." Minna put in optimistically. "Remember, Amos said he liked us."

Mrs. Salita dabbed the tablecloth with a napkin. "Amos is a good boy, really. You wait and see, he will try to make it up to you somehow. Just like that punctual son in the Bible…"

Robert stifled a laugh. "You mean the prodigal son?"

"Yes, that's what I meant, the probable son." Mrs. Salita declared.

"I believe the Lord will show us what to do to win them over. I try to just trust Him in this." Robert said. "Believe me, I've come to the place many times where I need more grit and grace than there is in me."

"This has happened before?" Minna asked.

"Grumblings. I have heard some things. Right now, though, I believe the Lord is telling me to go lay down! Do you have a cup of aspirin, Minna?"

"A cup of aspirin?" Minna tugged on her good ear.

"A couple. A couple of aspirin."

"Oh. Yes, I think I can spare a couple of aspirin."

***

Laguna

Sunday, June 17th

Dear David,

Thank you for the package with the jam. I often have crackers and they will taste so much better with something sweet from home.

I wonder if you have any string or light-weight paper you could send my way? I think I would like to try to make some kites to amuse the boys here in the village. It would be a good way to keep them out of Miss Cagle's hair.

Give my love to all.

Your brother,
Robert

FIVE

Sa mia-an-yi shra-tsak shrku-tra-nyi
(He Restoreth My Soul.)

Monday morning Minna was standing in front of the schoolhouse door scanning the road for any sign of approaching children when two little girls came high stepping up to her, all smiles. They had a chicken with them! The little one hollered, *"Goo-wa-goo!* Look, *Goo-wa-goo!"* Then she proceeded to cluck just in case Minna didn't get it. *Law me! A chicken on a leash!* They had managed to tie a string around the chicken's neck and the amazing thing was apparently the chicken had no objection.

Minna was so happy that any of the children came after the events of the day before, she couldn't see any way of disallowing the chicken in the school room. She saw Robert's eyes widen when he saw what they were bringing in. Minna noticed he kept up a steady supply of treats for the little girls all morning, especially for the little sister.

They accepted everything he gave them with many smiles and fed some of it to the chicken. It seemed to Minna perhaps it was smiling too, as much as a chicken can.

As soon as the little one finished one treat or even laid it down, Robert hustled over to give her another and after awhile Minna became mystified as to why.

"Does your chicken bite?" she asked the older girl, to which she replied, "Not much."

Minna found it difficult to keep the children's attention and it wasn't the chicken. It seemed each time she turned her back, when she turned again they were both trying to see out the window. Something was brewing!

The oldest of the two asked, "When we finish?"

"Are you going somewhere?"

"*Hah*. Today is throw up."

Surely Minna had heard incorrectly!

"Grow up?"

"No. Today is throw up over to Concho's!"

"Are they sick over there?"

"No! You know, grab day! You should go Miss Minna, you maybe grab something. You too, Robert."

Robert came to the schoolroom side of the building. "It is kind of like a birthday party Minna," he offered. "They go up on the roof of the house and toss goodies off to anyone below. If you catch something, it is yours to keep."

"My, my. Well, I guess you don't want to miss that," Minna mused.

Both little girls begged her to come too and pulled at her and Robert's arms until they agreed to go.

They walked along together, allowing the little girls and their chicken to skip on ahead.

"Robert, I was wondering, why so generous with the treats this morning? Was it because I had so few children attend?"

"Listen to the voice of experience," he said with a grin, "the chicken doesn't bite, but I can testify that the little sister does!"

"Bites? You mean as in bites people?"

"Yes, I was leading in prayer once at a service their whole family attended. We had all bowed our heads and as I led in prayer I had my arms behind me and my hands folded when little one came up behind me and left a nice set of tooth marks in my hand!"

Law me!

There was a large gathering crowd at Concho's, much laughter and a party atmosphere. Minna could see a young couple ascending a ladder that was propped against the wall of their house. They were taking many tubs and buckets up there with them. She couldn't see what was in the containers.

Robert said behind his hand, "Don't worry if you get some water on you. It is a blessing. They are hoping for rain."

"Water?" Just as she said it a water balloon burst at her feet and she jumped back.

"Sorry, I didn't warn you sooner!" Robert said with a laugh. Much yelling ensued as things began to tumble off the roof of the house. It was mostly food stuffs and kitchen gadgets. Robert caught a toy water pistol, fully loaded. "Here you go," he pushed it into Minna's hand just as another water balloon landed between them.

"What do I do with this?" Minna asked.

"It's a party." Robert shrugged. "Do what you like."

So Minna squirted him.

Robert took his glasses off and exchanged them with his handkerchief in his pocket. He wiped his face, "That's the idea!"

They both got into the spirit of things then. Minna caught a box of jello and a rubber spatula. Robert, a whistle and some hard candy.

Robert was proud of Minna. He noticed she was in a water pistol battle with some of the teenage boys, all giggling at the fun of it.

She may win them over yet, he thought.

In all the party atmosphere no one seemed to notice the dark clouds rolling in. The wind picked up and a rumble came from the heavens. As the first drops fell, Minna looked skyward. It had worked! They were getting the rain they had hoped for! No one minded the increasing deluge. They were wet already. Still, lightening is something else entirely. She ran back to Mrs. Salita's.

Minna slipped her shoes off at the door in case they might be muddy and tip-toed inside. She was just ready to call out so that Mrs. Salita would know she was home, but she heard something that stopped her. It sounded like crying.

"*A-moo. A-moo.*" It was Mrs. Salita's voice comforting someone. Minna strained to hear, leaning into her good ear. It was Gloria! Should she offer assistance? No, Gloria was with her mother. They needed their privacy. Minna quietly slipped into her room to change out of her wet things.

***

"*A-moo. A-moo.*" Mrs. Salita cooed at her daughter, patting her shoulder.

"If he would just listen to me!"

"I know. I know."

"I have tried. You know I have tried, but he just keeps doing the same things over and over and he doesn't care if it hurts me."

"Shhh. I know." *Well, if that isn't just like a man!*

"I tell him, he is married now. He shouldn't be looking at other women."

"That's right Gloria, he shouldn't." *Maybe the problem really is, the women are looking at him! Like that Miss Pynchon throwing herself at Robert!*

"I should have married Eddie."

That's right! Women would never be looking at that dog-faced boy!

"Can I stay here tonight, *Naya*? I just can't face him like this."

"Of course. Minna won't mind sharing her room with you."

"I can help you, Mama. It is a good time to pound some clay and make potteries!"

"Yes, yes. That is best."

Mrs. Salita took some blankets off a shelf and handed them to Gloria. "I think I heard Minna come in. Take these and make a pallet bed on the floor in her room. You can ask her where to put it out of her way."

Now who am I to be giving marital advice, Mrs. Salita thought grimly. *I have had three husbands and couldn't live with any of them! Looks like I better take some time off from matchmaking and concentrate on my own family for awhile. On the other hand, it would be good to get Robert over here to council Gloria…*

***

There was a good crowd of children the next morning in the schoolroom, fourteen counting the chicken! Robert had left early

55

because he needed to have some work done on the toodlelooka. Albert came about the same time as the children and spent the morning sitting in a folding chair leaning up against a wall, mostly sleeping.

Just as Minna was about to dismiss the children, Robert returned and told her he had to take the car all the way to Rio Pureo because there was a dog in the nose.

"A dog in the nose?"

"A clog. A clog in the hose," he corrected her.

"Oh, for the toodlelooka!"

Albert jumped up from his chair against the wall. "*Kenuty,* I was wondering if you and *Dyety* would mind if I borrow the schoolroom for my birthday this Saturday?"

Robert had an amused expression. "You still having birthdays my friend?"

Albert grunted. "I know. I know. Seems I've had more than my share. *Hah.* Here in Laguna, though, the birthday person does all the cooking for their party and they are the ones giving the presents to the guests."

"Sounds like a lot of work. Can we help?"

"Thought I'd set up tables outside the schoolhouse here and use the buck stove for some of the cooking." Albert's expression was guardedly hopeful. "It would be a lot easier if I had the use of your landlady's kitchen, *Dyety,* but…"

Minna grinned. "Okay, leave it to me, I'll ask her."

***

Robert admired the landscape through the windshield. What a wide turquoise sky! It was brilliant against the sand, rock and sage. There was a cloud or two, always a welcome sight in case one of them held even a drop of rain. He was driving Albert to Albuquerque for his birthday supplies.

His eyes darted sideways as he wondered just how old Albert would be. Albert had never said. Would it be impolite to ask? Probably so. Albert seemed to be dozing.

There was a lone figure plodding along the highway up ahead, head down, thumb held out.

"Land sakes!" Robert exclaimed as they passed the figure. "I believe that's Roland." He pulled the toodlelooka over and waited for the young man to catch up.

Roland bent over to look at the driver.

"*Ga-wa-tse,* Roland! Where you headed?"

"Back to Santa Fe. My leave is up."

"I can get you as far as Albuquerque."

"That'll do." Roland threw his duffle in the back seat. Then climbed in himself.

"*Ga-wa-tse, niash-che-uh.*" he said to Albert.

Albert opened his eyes and blinked at Roland. "*Eh-hiay,* Roland! I heard you were dead!"

"Dead?" Roland's expression registered surprise. "Nope. Not so's I noticed. Dead drunk maybe…" he laughed mirthlessly. "Oh. Sorry Reverend," he added.

Robert glanced over his shoulder. Roland didn't seem intoxicated to him. There was no odor of alcohol this time.

"My friend, I'm glad to see you are feeling better today."

"*Hah.*" Roland gazed out the window as they pulled back on the highway.

"How is your wife?"

"Doing okay. We had hoped the twins would be born while I was on leave, but guess they had other plans. She'll be coming to Albuquerque soon to stay with relatives until they are born."

"I am sorry you can't be here with her for that."

"Me too."

"I will be happy to give her a ride to Albuquerque when she is ready to come," Robert added.

"*Da-wa-eh,* Robert, but we have someone over to Acoma has already arranged to do that."

Albert opened one eye and closed it again, smiling. He was nodding his head.

***

Saturday, June 23rd

"Don't be *hiashpelinyi*. Slow poke!" Minna heard Mrs. Salita scolding Leon as she handed him a steaming pot of corn. "*Schu-troo!* Hurry up!"

Pot after pot went from the top of Mrs. Salita's stove out to the plaza where a long table had been set up.

Minna had participated in the cooking as well, attempting her mother's Double Delight Coconut Cream Cake. Somehow it did not turn out even singly delightful. The last time Minna had attempted this cake it was for Ernest Leigh and Frank before they shipped out to war. She finished the last of the icing and observed it with her head cocked to one side. *It didn't look any better that time either.*

"Oh dear*!*" She murmured.

Mrs. Salita stood next to her and patted her arm. "*We-meh.* That's all right. That old pole cat will eat it if it is sweet. He won't care what it looks like." She handed Minna one of the pots of chili. "Take this out and go see if Robert is back from the store."

"That's nearly everything. Aren't you coming out now?"

"*Uts-kia-sheh,*" Mrs. Salita said. "I will after awhile."

Minna took the chili to the loaded up tables and poked her head in the school- house door.

Albert sat next to the buck stove by himself with his hands folded in his lap. It was uncommonly hot in there with the stove fired up. He was waiting for some lamb stew to heat on top of the buck stove. The aroma was wonderful.

"*Ga-wa-tse* and happy birthday!" Minna greeted him.

"*Ga-wa-tse.*" Albert nodded her way, then looked beyond her as Robert came in.

"Hello, Robert. Anything I can do to help in here?" Minna asked.

"No, no. Things are well in hand. I see you have found the birthday boy!"

Robert brought in the groceries. There were several melons, tea and coffee, some cans of hominy and many cans of biscuits. Albert was stirring his stew.

"That sure smells good!" Robert exclaimed. "Is it rabbit?"

"No, it's lamb. I haven't had much luck rabbit hunting lately."

"Oh, hunting rabbits is easy…" Robert said dryly. "You just hide behind a rock and make a noise like a carrot."

Albert had no reply but a smile played across his face as he remained there, sitting and stirring.

BANG! Robert and Minna both ducked.

Albert kept stirring and calmly looked up at the ceiling.

The canned biscuits had become too warm on the buck stove and had exploded. Now biscuits were sprayed across the schoolroom ceiling, stuck fast!

Robert whistled. "Well, I believe the can did say 'popping fresh'," he said.

Mrs. Salita's worried face appeared in the door.

"Did someone shoot off a gun in here?"

Robert and Minna both pointed upward at the biscuits arranged on the ceiling.

"*Eh-hiay!* It is manna from heaven!"

Obligingly a couple of biscuits fell from the ceiling directly into the pot of stew. Albert looked up and then back at the pot.

"Dumplings," he said. "Old family recipe!"

***

Minna noted that there were a great many people at the party. Even Gloria and Leon were there and seemed to have patched things up somehow. They were sitting at one of the long tables eating together amiably. Robert was enjoying himself, joking with everyone in English and in Keresan. Minna noticed one or two of the students, some of the younger ones, peering at her shyly around their parents at the table. She picked up a spoon and showing it to the children, she huffed a breath on it and proceeded to hang it from her nose. The children collapsed in giggles. Minna pretended innocence.

Albert was handing out small gifts, just as he had said he would. He gave Robert a hand carved sling shot. Minna's gift was

59

shoe inserts made out of doe skin. *Better than cardboard! How did he know?*

Mrs. Salita kept a close watch on which dishes were hers. As they emptied, she sent Gloria and Leon into the kitchen with them. They volunteered to do the dishes and were doing so without any argument.

All of the other dishware belonged to Albert. Mrs. Salita instructed loudly all of those dishes should go in Robert's automobile.

"You don't mind do you Robert? Albert could use a ride back to New Laguna."

"No, I don't mind."

"Oh, I want to send some of that 'sinus restorative' soup to Albert's mother. Minna, would you bring it from the kitchen?"

As she did so, Mrs. Salita asked sweetly, "Have you met Albert's mother?"

"No, I…"

"Robert, you should take Minna along. I'm sure Delitha would like to meet her."

"Would you like to go?" Robert paused over his chicken leg.

"Well, I…"

"Here, take this too." Mrs. Salita piled a dish towel full of bread on top of the pot of soup.

Minna managed to get the soup and bread to the automobile without spilling. She settled inside with the soup and bread on her lap. Albert and Robert pushed the toodlelooka backward until it was pointed in the right direction. Minna resigned herself into the car seat.

Albert's mother was so small in her easy chair, she looked like a little brown elf. She had her legs propped up on a stool and was wrapped in a colorful shawl. Her hair was in one grey braid down her back. Her eyes appeared small and milky but her face was surprisingly smooth. Minna thought she must be absolutely ancient but could not fathom a guess as to her age.

"*Gawatse, baba,*" Robert said softly and patted her hand. "It's me, Robert, and I have the summer school teacher here with me, this is Miss Cagle."

"*Gawatse, baba.*" Minna said, not knowing what else to do. "Please call me Minna," she added.

Albert's mother smiled and reached out. Minna presumed she wanted to touch her so she offered both her hands to her.

"You are a hard worker," she said and Minna blushed that she had noticed how rough her hands were. "And unmarried..." she remarked, feeling for a ring and finding none. Delitha sighed heavily. "I am glad the council at Old Laguna has decided to reopen the school. When I was young I was sent to Indian school in Santa Fe where they punished us if we spoke Keresan."

"I am sorry they did that, Grandmother." Minna said. "When I was in school in the cove, the teachers used to whack our hands with a ruler if we said "ain't" or "hit is a nice day.""

Delitha was still holding Minna's hands and she squeezed them before she let go. "English is perhaps an unforgiving language," the old lady said.

Robert spoke again, "I can confirm that the children are teaching Miss Cagle as much Keresan as she is teaching them English."

"That is good. Keresan is not a written language so English has its usefulness." Delitha settled back in her chair. "Albert, I am feeling better, is there soup?"

Albert hastened to get a bowl for her, then dismissed Robert and Minna with many thanks.

"I hope she did not offend you, Minna." Robert said when they had returned to the toodlelooka.

"No, indeed. I found her very sweet."

"She is that."

They drove on in silence for a bit. After awhile Minna had a flash of inspiration.

"Robert, does Albert's mother read Braille?"

***

The next Monday Minna was dismayed to discover that no one had come for lessons. "I wonder if they are staying away because of the unhappy council members?"

"We shouldn't assume that yet. It could be everyone went to an all tribal gathering. They sometimes have those in various places here in New Mexico."

Minna waited a couple of hours and to keep busy she helped Robert dust and sweep and straighten up the schoolhouse. They talked about going to see Mrs. Day for another language lesson, but Robert could not find the hymnal he used. Both of them searched high and low but could not find it, nor even one single hymnal that he had in English. He could have misplaced one but surely not all of them.

"I hate to say it," Robert said dejectedly. "In light of recent events, I have to suspect vandalism."

Minna was glad she had kept her books in her room at Mrs. Salita's.

They were both feeling pretty discouraged, and doubly so when the next day it became clear Minna wasn't going to have any lessons that day either. After waiting a couple of hours, she asked, "Could I have a ride to Albuquerque? I want to discuss this with Miss Pynchon."

"Certainly! I should probably have a word with the home mission board as well."

***

Miss Pynchon peered over her stylish glasses.

"I'm not overly concerned Melissa. The council has been very implicit on their desire to use the schoolhouse in the matter we have discussed."

"Minna. It's Minna."

"Er, yes. Minna. Did Mr. Carlisle bring you to Albuquerque?" Miss Pynchon crossed the room to gaze out the window of her office. Minna could not help noticing her expensive looking sling back heels. Minna pushed her own feet under her chair, hoping Miss Pynchon had not observed her own scuffed and worn shoes.

"Yes, he has been very helpful to me and my work. Even when I have had only two students." Minna smiled at the memory.

"Two students and their pet chicken," she added.

That got Miss Pynchon's attention. "Did you say chicken?"

Miss Pynchon's face took on the sour expression Minna had come to associate with her. Like a glass of lemonade without the sugar.

"Miss Cagle! You must not allow the children to bring livestock into the class room!"

Without the sugar or the water for that matter. Just sour lemons and maybe ice cubes!

Minna folded her lips between her teeth, stifling a giggle.

"Yes, Miss Pynchon. Uh...I guess I'd better go."

"Yes, Millicent, I think you'd better. I'm very busy and I need to leave soon for Santa Fe. Give my regards to Mr. Carlisle. Please tell him the next time he is in Albuquerque perhaps he could join me for lunch."

"It's Minna!" *Law me!*

***

Minna clutched her mail to her heart, as well as the copy of the Braille alphabet she had purchased at a bookstore in Albuquerque. She had plans for a project with the children when they came back for lessons. *If they do come back*!

She was thinking about the headlines she had seen on a newspaper in the bookstore. **U.S. ARMY AND MARINES COMPLETE CAPTURE OF OKINAWA!** *Surely the war will be over soon!* Her letter from home was burning in her heart and in her hand. Dare she even read it? What if it is even worse news? Apparently something else was burning. The automobile sputtered and smoke streamed out of the hood.

"Eh-Hiay!" Robert exclaimed in Keresan. He pulled over in what seemed to Minna like the middle of nowhere. Grabbing the handkerchief out of his pocket, he used it to lift the hood of the toodlelooka. "It's the radiator, Minna. I always carry water to add when this happens! I will have to let it cool off a bit first though. Why don't you wait over there in the shade until I can get us up and running again."

While Robert fussed with the toodlelooka, Minna sat down in the sand under a little scruffy tree big enough to afford a little shade. She decided she would be brave enough to look at the mail she had collected in Albuquerque.

Sweetwater
June 20

Dear Minerva,

We have heard that Ernest Leigh is being sent home. We don't exactly know what his condition is, but he is expected to be placed in the hospital in Knoxville. Your Pa and me are going there to be with him on the 22nd.

We knew you would want to know. Hope you are well.

Love,
Your Ma

Minna's mind went all awhirl. How badly was Ernest Leigh hurt? What of Frank? Had he been wounded as well? How could she stand another day until she knew all of the details? She felt truly afraid.

When they finally got the automobile running again Minna was overly quiet the rest of the trip back.

"I was able to speak to my directors at the Home Mission board in Albuquerque." Robert seemed to not notice how distracted she was. "They have said I should carry on as I have until I am asked to leave. Hopefully that won't happen. Guess I am feeling somewhat comforted about it. How about you Minna?" Robert asked as they came into Laguna. Preoccupied with her own thoughts, she didn't answer.

"Are you all right Miss Cagle?"

SIX

Ke shku-i-oots ia-e he-an-yi da-wa tse-e-shro e ga-she
go-dzi-nye-uh
(He Leadeth Me In The Paths Of Righteousness
For His Name's Sake.)

Robert listened with full attention. This was a side of Minna he had not seen before. She had told him in a trembling voice about the letter and her concerns for her brother.

"I can certainly relate to how you must be feeling. I had many agonizing moments of worry over my own brother when he was in harms way in Europe. I can only assure you of God's love for both you and your brother. That He will be with you both whatever lays ahead." *Ah, but that isn't what she wants to hear, is* it? *She wants assurance that her brother will be all right.*

Robert often thought his training in seminary inadequate for counseling during times of war."And there's something else," Minna revealed reluctantly. "Ernest Leigh's best friend is in the same unit. He is very special to me. I had hoped we would marry after the war. Now I'm not even sure if he is still alive."

A sweetheart. How could he not have known? Robert tried not to let his surprise be evident. Even if she had never made mention of it before, it stood to reason a young woman as lovely as…well, best not to think of possibilities any more. She was evidently spoken for, and that was that! Still, it grieved his heart a little, if only…

Robert shook his head. "Would you like to pray with me about it," he said gently.

"Oh…I…no, I just don't feel I have the words to express…" Minna's voice trailed off.

65

"Miss Cagle, can I show you something? It might help. Come walk with me."

She came willingly. Little did she know it wasn't just a walk, it was a difficult climb. They snaked their way up the side of the mesa all the way to the top. Once there the view was magnificent! Robert found it more awesomely beautiful every time he went up there. Always more spectacular than the time before.

From the top of the mesa you could see a multitude of colorful miles. The earth lit up from a heavenly spot light and to the west, the landscape was in deep shadow. It looked like the earth had been sliced with a precision knife, revealing layers of every color. In one portion of an expansive sky, clouds gave evidence of a rainstorm, and there was a faint rainbow on the horizon.

"I come up here often to think and pray. It usually helps me put things into perspective," Robert said.

"It's like you can see back to the beginning of time," Minna whispered.

"Indeed. And up here don't you get the feeling that God is big enough to handle all our problems if we trust him to do so?"

"I want to trust Him. I guess I don't have enough faith. I just don't know sometimes if I can hang on any longer."

"I believe faith is not hanging on. Faith is being willing to let go. Just trusting."

"Even if I'm left all alone?"

She turned to him and he felt a catch of breath. What a beautiful woman she was, standing there on the rock on the very precipice! The way the breeze lifted her scarf from her shoulders she looked like an angel. *Heaven help me!*

"You are never alone, Minna. Let me show you something else…" Robert took her by the hand and they picked through the rocks until they came to a sizeable hole in the side of the rock wall. A cave! Just as they were about to go further, they were startled by an explosion of beating wings. Bats!

To his embarrassment, Robert screamed like a little girl. They both crouched with their arms over their heads until the deluge was past. Robert's heart was beating so hard it gave him a headache.

66

"Oh, Miss Cagle I'm so sorry. I didn't know about the bats. Are you all right?"

"Yes, I think so," she gasped.

Minna started laughing and she couldn't stop. Big fat tears rolled down her cheeks and every time Robert thought she was back in control, another round of giggles came up out of her.

"You stay here and let me make sure there aren't any others." Robert picked up a stone and heaved it into the cave opening then quickly crouched back down. "Well, there now, don't you feel better?" Robert offered his hand and Minna got up off her knees and followed him inside the cave.

"Here is what I wanted you to see before the Lord saw fit to make you laugh."

Minna paused at the thought. *Is that what happened?*

Robert showed her a place in the rock wall where figures had been chiseled out by ancient hands. There was a life size shape of a human hand, a crescent moon and what may have been a sun. Minna instinctively covered the figure with her own hand and it fit perfectly.

"They are called petroglyphs," Robert said. "They are all over the rock country here in the west and are very ancient. I've been told if there is a picture with a hand in front of it like this one, it means the person who carved the picture was expressing the desire to have the object that follows it. A crescent moon depicts a change or something new, and the sun probably means they are hoping for a happy outcome."

Robert ran his hand over the entire piece of art work. "When I look at something this old it reminds me that we all have had our desires and our challenges and our prayers. God understands that. If we allow him to show us what is best for us we can trust him, even if the answers to our prayers come in an unexpected form. You are not alone Minna. There is all of humanity that shares that challenge. That is the challenge of trust."

Robert smiled softly. "I too, share that challenge. Believe me, there have been times when I questioned everything. I come up here and I see how God uses the light and the shadow to make the whole something extraordinarily beautiful. Do you see what I mean?"

***

Minna lay tossing and turning most of the night. When was it that she gave up the desire to pray? At last she drifted off into the dream. The dream that was all too real...

"Ma'un! Ma'un!"

"It's all right, honey. I'm here with you."

She felt her grandfather's big work worn hands patting her arms, smoothing the sweat drenched sheets around her.

"No! I want ma'un!"

"She can't come right now honey. She needs to stay in Townsend. The babies are too little and fragile to bring home to all this sickness."

"I want Ma'un," she whimpered. It was just too much effort to cry anymore. She drifted back into that wavy place. The place where there was a constant roar in her left ear and a pounding in her head. The place where there was a knife in her throat each time she swallowed and at least three more in her stomach. She swam back to the surface and found there was a cold wet cloth on her head. Grandpa Joe had left the room. She was alone with Sissy, sharing the sick bed. She sat bolt upright. Sissy! Her younger sister looked so pale and still! Was she dead? Frantically she shook her little sister with what little strength she had left.

"Sissy! Sissy!"

The little girl opened bleary eyes. "Ma'un?" she whispered.

They both heard the church bells tolling another death in the cove.

"Please God! Don't take anybody else! Please God!"

Her little sister was doubled over with another fit of coughing. Blood was trickling from her nose...

Minna sat upright in bed, just as she had all those years ago. She rubbed her bad ear, remembering the pain. *Why were you deaf to us that time, Lord? All those deaths in the cove from typhoid fever...*

Minna put her feet to the floor and padded over to the window. The stars were especially bright. She could almost feel their warmth. So many stars!

So what was this business of praying? Minna thought about the panoramic vista up on the mesa. This view of the stars in the New Mexico sky was just as majestic. *It must be what they mean when they say "the big picture."* That had been Robert's point, how it illustrated that all the pieces fit together somehow. The good and the bad. The dark and the light. She thought about the bat cave and how she had instinctively covered the petroglyph with her hand. Palm to ancient palm. Like hands in prayer. *Maybe I've been praying all along and didn't know it!*

Okay, Lord. I am putting Ernest Leigh and Frank in your hands now. But please, if you could just send one of your angels to see Frank through the war. Please see that Ernest Leigh heals of his wounds! Please Lord, if you don't mind, help me do what I need to here. Help me fit into the big picture...

***

Laguna
June 27

Dear Folks,

Thank you for letting me know about Ernest Leigh. Please let me know of his progress. Tell him I wish I could be there to help you care for him. I am praying for his full recovery.

I am doing what I was sent here to do and I am longing for the day I can return home.

I love you and miss you all,
Minna

***

Robert smiled approvingly at the scene in the schoolroom. Minna had made a large chart of the English alphabet and the corresponding braille dots. The children had dictated stories which Minna had written in large block letters on sheets of paper in English. Now the children were using toothpicks to punch the braille dots that matched each letter. Minna had told them the pages would be sewn together to make a book of their stories for Albert's mother, Delitha.

The children were very enthusiastic about their project, but none more so than Robert. *What a lovely idea! What a lovely woman! I hope this boy she is promised to has some idea how fortunate he is.*

***

Robert thought the commotion he heard outside was the usual disturbance from the usual teenage boys. Then he recognized Gloria's voice, high pitched and angry. He looked out the window in time to see her chasing Leon with a stick!

Robert hurried outside.

When Gloria saw Robert exiting the school building she threw the stick down in a huff and hurried into her mother's house, slamming the door.

Leon greeted Robert sheepishly, "*Ga-wa-tse*, Robert."

"Do you need any help?"

"I uh, guess I need a ride to my sister's place at Acomita if you are free."

"I'll get my keys."

They drove in silence for some time until Leon finally said, "My sister is staying with relatives in Albuquerque until the twins are born. She won't mind if I stay at their place in Acomita for awhile."

Robert knew it would be impolite to ask questions, but it troubled him that things had gotten this far out of hand again. He knew Leon would tell him eventually.

"Gloria needs some time to think things over, I think." Leon offered.

"Is there anything I can do, Leon?"

"Just a ride to Acomita maybe."

***

Minna found to her dismay that she was only half listening to Gloria's tirade against Leon. She was sitting on the edge of the bed while Gloria brushed her hair and gave her an ear full. Minna didn't know what to say. She wanted to be a friend to Gloria, but she had never noticed any of the things she was saying about Leon. Yes, he was a handsome man to be sure. Maybe she had noticed the other women looking at him at Albert's birthday party, but she had not noted any effort on his part to encourage them to do so. Finally Gloria took a breath and Minna was able to get a word in after all.

"What does Robert say?"

Gloria shrugged and looked away. "He thinks I should trust more."

Ah, sounds familiar.

"And he thinks I should pray about it."

"And what do you think of his advice?"

"Well, I tried that. Praying that is. Maybe I still have trouble trusting."

"I see." *Well, we have something in common then!* "I hope you can work it out Gloria. It would be sad to think you were separating permanently."

Gloria pursed her lips. "It will depend on what Leon does now."

Dangerous! Men never seem to know what to do!

Minna found herself lost in thought about Frank. Didn't he realize how much she needed to hear from him? She knew it was difficult for him to write home, but Ernest Leigh managed it at least occasionally! Why hadn't Frank cared enough to write to her? Or at least send word through her brother to let her know he is all right! Minna went to bed with a new prayer on her mind.

Lord, could you please help Gloria and Leon through this? I think they deserve some happiness.

*　　　 ＊＊＊*

The following week, Minna found one day to be mostly like the next. Children came sporadically to the schoolroom, never the same ones from day to day. It made it difficult to build on any one lesson. It felt like each day she had to start over from the beginning.

Robert stayed out of the way and kept busy with his own work. On Thursday he had word from Albert that he was under the weather so Robert went to visit him.

Minna's project had finally taken shape. She sent a booklet of the children's stories in Braille for Albert's mother. When Robert came back, he had Albert in the toodlelooka.

He took Minna aside. "I am worried about Albert. I am taking him to Albuquerque to the doctor. Do you want to come along?"

"No. I'm expecting Miss Pynchon today. I'd better stay."

"Can I pick up anything for you in town?"

"Just my mail if there is time, thank you. Oh, can you wait just a minute?" She hurried to fetch the letter she had written for the folks at home and another post card to Frank. "Could you mail these for me?" Minna was grateful for Robert's thoughtfulness. Maybe there would be a miracle and her mail could hold a letter from Frank!

***

"What is this?" Miss Pynchon looked over her pearly rimmed glasses at the chart Minna had used for the Braille project.

Minna rubbed her ear nervously. "Just a little project I did with the children."

"I don't understand. What are the dots?"

Oh, no! Here comes that sourpuss expression again!

"They are Braille letters. The children were helping me make a book of their stories for a blind lady at New Laguna."

"Marjorie! How many times must I tell you? You are not required to teach these children to read…just a basic understanding of English!"

"I thought it would be a way of making them familiar with the English alphabet. What is more basic than that?"

"Braille of all things! I just don't know if you are working out. I may have to report this to the supervisory board..."

"The project is done. I won't use it any more if you don't want me to. You know I haven't really been given any direction on what it is you want me to do here."

Miss Pynchon pursed her lips. "Don't be impertinent! Your instructions are simple. Get these children to be able to converse in English. That is all!"

Miss Pynchon picked up her belongings and stomped to the door, pausing briefly at Robert's privacy curtain to peek around it. Finding no one there she flounced out.

Minna whispered, "It's Minna, not Marjorie..."

***

Minna was helping Mrs. Salita and Gloria with the dishes when she heard the toodlelooka pull up next door. She looked out the window and was surprised to see that Albert had not returned with Robert. Robert came to the door holding his hat in his hands.

"I left Albert at the hospital. They want to keep him a few days to run tests. I thought you would want to know."

"I hope they will be able to find some way to make him feel better." Minna said sincerely.

"I also inquired about Leon's sister. She has given birth to the twins but one of them was much smaller than the other. They are keeping the babies at the hospital until they are stronger."

Just like my little brother and sister, years ago! Minna's brother and sister were already two months old when her mother thought it was safe enough to bring them home. That fateful day Minna and her little sister were weak from having had Typhoid fever and Minna was already having difficulty with her ear. Yet it had been a happy time for her family. A time the whole family had begun to heal.

"I thought I would drive over to Acomita and let Leon know the latest."

Minna wondered if Robert would ask her to go to Acomita with him. He seemed to hesitate to say anything further. He kept turning his hat over and over in his hands. *What are you trying to say?*

"I picked up your mail." Robert handed her a newspaper. Minna noted the headlines: **GENERAL MACARTHUR ANNOUNCES LIBERATION OF THE PHILIPPINES!** Robert withdrew a single letter from inside his hat and gave it to Minna. "I hope it is good news," he said.

SEVEN

*Had, tu-yu-ma esh-chi-mi dye-ka e-wa se-nyitr-dye-ya, tsa-dze
no-wa-shchi-shkoo-nu, sche siu-to-nyi ia-e
sep-shro-yu-wi shra-apshe*
(Yea, though I walk through the valley of the shadow of death, I
will fear no evil, for thou art with me.)

Robert wished Minna had gone with him to Albuquerque. The trip back had seemed interminably long and lonesome! Still, maybe it was better she hadn't. He might not be able to keep her from guessing he was attracted to her. She was spoken for! Maybe the letter was from her young man. He had thought about it all the way back from Albuquerque and now his troubled thoughts plagued him all the way to Acomita. He truly was a lonely man. He realized that now. Not that he could do anything about it!

He had come into this work willingly, even eagerly. Surely it was exactly what he felt the Lord was leading him to do! He figured it would be a rare woman indeed that would agree to the hardships he faced living the way he did. No, even if she were free to do so, how could he even contemplate asking Minna to stay here? It was clear that she looked forward to fulfilling her obligations in New Mexico and then returning home. If only he had more to offer someone like her. Someone exactly like her! *Oh, stop it! Stop! Stop! STOP!* Robert threw on the brakes as a coyote slinked across the road in front of him. Robert blinked at the skinny old beast. The old trickster appeared to be grinning.

***

Minna stared at the letter in her hand. It was from her sister and it was worrisome. Sissy described their brother since he came

75

home from the war. In her words, he was a "broken man." " *His leg has been shattered and he barely can walk but that is not the worst of it. Mostly he just sits and stares out the window. He never smiles. At night he has terrible nightmares and it is hard to wake him up from them. He answers us when we ask him questions but he has no further conversation. None of us know how to help him.*"

Minna just didn't know what to do. Should she go home? How would that help? She ached in her heart for him. Ernest Leigh, that had always had a smile, a joke and more than a few pranks when they were growing up together. What would become of him now?

Minna searched through her belongings for something to write a letter. She would send it through Sissy and that way if Ernest Leigh didn't feel like reading it, she knew Sissy would read it to him. She yanked the notebook out of her bag that she had been using to write the children's stories. She flipped through the simple stories the children had dictated. Many of them were quite humorous. These were the stories she had helped them translate into Braille for Albert's mother. Albert's mother had enjoyed them, maybe Ernest Leigh would as well. *Out of the mouths of babes.*

Minna selected a few of the most endearing ones and added a note of encouragement of her own. She fashioned an envelope out of a paper grocery sack and addressed it. Perhaps Robert could mail it when he went to Albuquerque to visit Albert. She brought the package to her lips. *Please Lord, let it do some good!*

Then she scribbled on the post card she had bought the last trip to Albuquerque.

Dear Frank, Please write. Please. Love, Minna

***

The following Monday Minna was in the midst of her lessons when Leon came to the schoolhouse and requested a word with Robert. She could see them in earnest conversation each time she glanced out the schoolroom window. How she hoped it meant Leon was getting back together with Gloria! She tried to have faith. To trust! But she could tell by the expression on Robert's face when he slipped back inside, that the news was not good.

Robert did something he had never done before. He interrupted her lesson and asked to have a word with her outside. Minna pulled out some crayons and paper and got the students started on a picture story, then joined Robert and Leon outside the school house.

"Yes, what is it?" She looked back and forth between them.

"Minna, Leon and I want to ask an enormous favor of you." Robert seemed to be having difficulty keeping the emotion out of his voice. "That is, Leon and I and his family. You see, he hesitates to ask for Gloria's help at this time. We both feel a woman's touch is needed…" His voice trailed off.

"Yes, of course I'll help. Whatever it is." Minna offered.

Leon spoke up. "It is my sister Emma that needs your help *Dyety*. She has lost one of the twins. It was born too small and too weak to survive."

Minna gasped ,"Oh, Leon, no!"

Leon swallowed and continued, " I have asked Robert to take me to Albuquerque and give Emma a ride back home. We feel having a woman along will be a comfort to her. I would have asked my wife but…"

Oh my! Minna's heart felt like it would burst. The poor mother! Poor Leon! How could Minna do this? What could she say?

"Of course I'll help. Let me dismiss the children for the day and we can get started right away."

***

Minna hated everything about the hospital. The antiseptic smell, the sterile colors, the cold hard corridors. There was no comfort here. She wanted to help but how could she face poor Emma? What could she possibly say? The death of a little child must be the worst kind of pain a parent could endure. Especially with her husband away at war!

77

Minna had to think, what if she had married Frank before he went to war? She might have found herself in exactly this situation.

After a long wait, a nurse gathered Robert and Minna and led them into an office. She retreated for a short while but returned with Leon and Emma. Emma was holding the live twin. It was wrapped tightly in a receiving blanket. All Minna could see of the tiny baby was it's little face. So tiny! So precious! It's little nose and mouth pinched up and it's eyes tightly closed.

Leon had his arm protectively around Emma's shoulder. Minna could see the family resemblance. Emma had lovely features and smooth coppery skin. Her hair was cut in the typical Acoma ceremonial style, long in back and short on the sides. She reminded Minna of the paintings of native women she had admired in Santa Fe.

"This is Miss Cagle." Leon said to Emma, "We call her *Dyety*."

Emma looked at Minna and Minna managed a weak smile.

"And of course, you know *Kenuty*, Robert." Leon added.

Robert stood up. "Emma, please let us assist you in any way that brings you comfort," he said.

Emma said nothing but sat down gingerly.

The nurse returned and presented papers to sign. She left again and another person came into the office, an orderly. He was carrying a cardboard box. Minna realized to her horror that it contained the body of the dead twin.

Leon accepted the box from the orderly and Emma stood up.

"Do you want a wheelchair?" The orderly asked Emma. She slowly shook her head no.

"No thank you," Leon told the orderly. "She wants to walk."

Minna and Robert stood as well. She could see that Leon wanted to support Emma as she bravely exited the office but he was holding the box. Minna hoped she would not have to carry it, then scolded herself for being selfish. To her surprise Emma pushed the live twin into her arms.

"*Dyety*. Please." Emma said softly.

Minna looked down at the little baby in her arms. Such a precious little face! The baby already had a shock of fine black hair. He made a little cooing sound and Minna felt her heart melt. She found herself thinking in wonderment, *I already love this baby!* She smiled at the little face.

Emma reached for the box and cradled it in her arms. Minna swallowed the lump in her throat and set her jaw determinedly. *They don't need me to be emotional. I have to be strong!*

***

Robert kept biting his lip on the drive back. This was the hardest thing he had to do since coming to New Mexico. He glanced at Leon, who was riding up front with him. Leon's face was intense but his eyes were soft and damp.

Robert looked in his rear view mirror. He could hear Emma softly singing in Keresan. She was cradling the box and gently rocking back and forth.

"Dru-we-shatts samaq..."

"Good bye my daughter."

"E soow, E he-ko dzooshr..."

"Oh, dear, where are you going?"

"Naya, E sa-ma ehs tsoos..."

"Mother, I'm going home."

"Hah oo-wak. Yu-goos e-you..."

"Yes baby. Fly away!"

Robert saw that Minna was holding the live twin, a single tear rolling down her cheek. How he wanted to hold and comfort her! *Lord have mercy!*

The baby whimpered and Minna held its little face next to hers, cheek to cheek. "Shhhh. Shhhh." She whispered tenderly.

What a mother she would make!

It took longer than usual getting all the way out to Acomita village. Robert took the off roads very slowly, trying not to bump the passengers in the back seat. When they finally arrived at the adobe house where Leon had been staying, Robert was surprised to see Mrs. Salita and Gloria were there! He wondered how they knew to come and how they had arrived! The way they looked, perhaps they had walked!

Gloria descended on Emma openly crying and all of the women went into the house together. Leon shook hands with Robert and thanked him many times for his help. Then he took the baby out of Minna's arms and thanked her as well.

Robert understood. It was time for the family to mourn now. He and Minna should go back to Laguna. He drove back to Laguna in silence. Minna's tears were falling freely now. When they pulled up to Mrs. Salita's house she collapsed into his open arms sobbing.

"It's all right to cry Minna. Our tears help us to heal." Robert said gently. *"A-moo, a-moo."*

***

Mrs. Salita wearily opened the door to her house. Long shadows were forming to the east.

The sun sets on one life. A new life begins.

As she came into the house she heard the tea kettle whistling in her kitchen.

Dyety is making tea. That is good...

Mrs. Salita was surprised to see Minna was sitting at the kitchen table in the dark. She rescued the tea kettle and brought it to the table where she sat down heavily.

"More water?"

Minna slid her cup across the table and Mrs. Salita filled it with hot water. Even in the dark it was apparent that Minna's face was red and swollen.

Mrs. Salita brushed a stray tear from her own face and said matter-of-factly, "Gloria has gone back home with her husband. Seems this tragedy has caused them to rethink some things."

"It makes me hopeful that at least some good can come from this," Minna said wearily.

"Do you want something to eat?"

"No, thank you." Minna replied. "How did you get back home?"

"Leon borrowed the Sanchez truck."

They sat in silence for awhile. Mrs. Salita lit a lantern against the dark. "You know," she said, "Maybe I have been too hard on Leon." She smoothed her dress and shook her head. "When I saw how tenderly he cares for his sister… well, it made me hope he and Gloria will have children some day."

Minna smiled.

Mrs. Salita went on, "It is like Robert tries to tell us.. There is a blessing in all things. If you know where to look."

"Yes, I suppose so." Minna said softly. "If you know where to look."

***

The next morning Robert brought another letter. It was not from Frank.

It was a note hastily scratched on a grocery bag indicating in dismay that Miss Pynchon had come to observe Minna's class and had found no one there. It further indicated her intent to return the next day and her expectation of an explanation as to why there was no class to observe!

"I'm so sorry Minna, " Robert said. "I feel responsible for her ire. I will explain the situation to her when she comes. I'm sure she will understand under the circumstances."

Robert did just that. Minna noted wryly that when Miss Pynchon came, she spent far more time in conversation with Robert than in observation of her class.

"Well, I guess I have to let it go this time Molly. But as long as you realize your first responsibility is to the children."

Minna sighed. "Maybe you should call me *Dyety*."

Miss Pynchon frowned. "Too hard to remember nicknames."

***

Monday, July 16, 1945

Mrs. Salita dusted herself off and stamped the sand off of her shoes. She reached for the door to the schoolhouse several

81

times, then thought better of it. At last with a look of determination she opened the door a crack and said in a strong voice, "Robert?"

Minna appeared at the door. "Oh, Mrs. Salita it's you."

"*Hah,* I'm looking for Robert. I hope I'm not disturbing you. I waited until it looked like all the children had left."

"No, no. Come in if you like, but Robert isn't here. He left early this morning I think he took a load of passengers up to the sheep camp."

"Ah." Mrs. Salita sat down wearily on one of the folding chairs and mopped her face with a handkerchief.

"Is there anything I can do for you, Mrs. Salita?" Minna offered.

"No. no. I came to tell Robert I just got word my ex-husband has passed away."

Minna sat down abruptly. "Oh, no!"

Mrs. Salita went hurriedly on, "I came to ask Robert to say a few words at the funeral. There will be others to speak. His daughter by his first marriage is Catholic so she is asking the priest up at Acoma. Oh, and he was friends with a couple of Mormon elders so they will say something. Any one that comes will be allowed to speak if they want to."

"I'm sure Robert will want to do that. When is the funeral?"

"This afternoon." Mrs. Salita gulped. "We bury our dead quickly." She stood and straightened her dress. She was resolved to do this stoically. "I will wait for Robert over at the house. You will tell him when he gets back?"

"Of course." Minna patted Mrs. Salita's arm. "Is there anything I can do?"

"No, *Dyety.* Just tell Robert, please."

A couple of hours went by before Mrs. Salita saw Robert and Minna walking toward her house. It was a cloudy day so she brought her shawl as she came out to meet them. *Wouldn't it be something if it rained?*

Robert took her hands in his and seemed shaken. "Naya, I am sorry for your loss."

Mrs. Salita was speechless. It was evident Minna had been crying again. *How touching that they are so sympathetic!*

They entered Robert's automobile and Mrs. Salita directed them to the foot of the mesa at old Acoma, Sky City. "We will walk from here," Mrs. Salita said.

Minna took one arm and Robert the other as they escorted Mrs. Salita up the hill.

The road was steep and difficult where parts of it had washed away. Several cars brought up the rear of the procession. One of them became stuck in the sand and had to be pushed out.

Well, I am an old woman, but I can still walk! Guess it would be rude not to accept their help. There's his sister! I haven't seen her since the day we got married so long ago! Mrs. Salita embraced her and several other relatives. *Claudia looks terrible!* Mrs. Salita pulled her shawl up over her head so the relatives couldn't see her face. *Well, let's get this over with!*

The priest started things out and spoke about merits and good deeds. Mrs. Salita wasn't really paying attention as she was trying to think of what to say when her turn would come.

The Mormon elders were brief in their comments on what he had been like as a friend. Robert read the twenty third Psalm in Keresan, *Yus sa-pish-tu-ra...* The Lord is my shepherd...

What a nice touch. Mrs. Salita's eyes brightened. She knew just what she wanted to say!

Now the medicine man took his turn.

"All I can say is, I wish he had come to me instead of that nurse from the U.S. Indian Service. She thought she could cure him with Alka Seltzer and you see what that got him!"

Several of the women began weeping loudly.

This is getting too morbid! Good thing it is my turn.

Mrs. Salita cleared her throat several times and looked at Robert and Minna's supportive faces.

"Well, everyone knows he was my ex- husband and what kind of man he was," she said with conviction. "But I don't think of this body we are burying as him. It is just the shell of the man..." Mrs. Salita smiled mischievously, "It is just the shell...and the nut has gone to heaven!"

***

"I don't think they appreciated my contribution to the occasion," Mrs. Salita said in the toodlelooka on the way back to Laguna.

"It was perhaps a little unexpected," Robert said gently.

"I was just trying to lighten it up a little. You know, like the good book says, 'make do to others as they would make do to you.' Isn't that right?"

Robert nodded. "Close enough."

Well, at least it made Minna smile, Mrs. Salita thought smugly.

Just outside Laguna village Robert slammed on the brakes.

"Have Mercy!" He yelled.

Mrs. Salita peered out the window. "Oh, that's just Albert," she said matter of factly. "Guess he wants a ride."

Minna grabbed her stomach and looked like she had seen a ghost. Robert was in shock as well. Mrs. Salita looked back and forth between them. *What's wrong with them?*

"Minna, didn't you say Albert had passed?' Robert's eyes were wild.

"Y-yes. That's what I understood her to say. Wh-when she said her ex-husband had passed and I knew Albert had been sick. Oh!" Minna opened the car door and jumped out with a hug for a very surprised Albert.

"I thought you were dead!" she kept saying.

Mrs. Salita wagged her head back and forth. "Oh, Robert," she said. "Didn't you know I have had three husbands? *Eh-Hiay!*"

EIGHT

Ktra-tsish-ta-nyi shrkoo-tsa-yo.
(Thy rod and thy staff they comfort me)

"Heavenly Father," Robert began as he perched on a crop of boulders that overlooked the beautiful vista before him. "Your creation overwhelms me…"

He had come alone this time to pray up on the mesa, but the view with all it's majesty was not as lovely this time without Minna in it.

He squirmed uncomfortably and tried to get back on track. He had come for clarity, for guidance, not to fantasize.

Robert was aware of Mrs. Salita's matchmaking ploys and was amused by them. It was the people like her that so clearly demonstrated their love for him and their desire for his work to continue there with them that had kept him going thus far.

Was he making a difference? He hoped so, prayed so, desperately wanted to believe so, still… Should he stay? Should he doom himself to a life of loneliness? To say it was hard living like this was the prize winner of all understatements. And expecting someone else to embrace the same conditions was inconceivable! No, he couldn't impose that on anyone. Not Minna, not the very silly Miss Pynchon who he realized had a serious crush on him. Imagine someone like her living as he did! It was unthinkable.

Robert gazed out on the scene before him. *Look at this! Look at the enormity of it! How can I not trust You Lord to deliver me from my dilemma?* Robert crossed his arms over his chest and sighed. He was tempted to sit here all day. Here he wasn't on the verge of trying to persuade Minna to stay in New Mexico with him instead of returning home to that service boy. Up here he wasn't bothered by a misguided Miss Pynchon.

Just breathe the beauty in and get back to work! I can't make a difference up here. I have to go back for that. Mrs. Salita, Leon and Gloria, Albert (now alive again! I must do a sermon on Lazarus!) Robert smiled at that. He set his shoulders and stood up. *I will do what I can. The rest is up to you, Lord.*

Robert wound his way through the rock formations and only stopped for a moment for tradition's sake at the bat cave. *No bats today!* He gently placed his hand over the petroglyph hand, just as Minna had done the day he brought her up here.

As he started his descent off the mesa, he spied a feather adorned prayer stick upright among the rocks. He realized someone else had been praying up there.

***

Minna stood at the schoolroom window watching the dust rise off the Sanchez' truck as it pulled away from Mrs. Salita's house.

Leon and Gloria could often be seen riding in the borrowed truck together now. *Answered prayer!* Minna guessed it made Leon feel like the head of the household to drive Gloria places instead of asking Robert for a ride in the toodlelooka so frequently.

She felt little Maria Alvarez tugging on her skirt and looked down at her sweet upturned face and big brown eyes. The children had been quick to catch on that they needed to touch her to get her attention as they couldn't remember in which ear she could understand a question.

"Yes Maria?'

"Miss Minna. You be our teacher always?"

Minna felt her expression soften. "I-I can't say for sure, Maria. I only know they have asked me for the summer."

What would happen after that? So much depended on the end of the war. The end of the war! How she wished it would end! So much depended on Frank!

Minna sighed deeply and looked back out the window. She was beginning to think Frank couldn't be depended on. Maybe she would always be alone.

86

She forced herself to consider the possibility of staying on as the teacher in Laguna. The position had never been offered but if it were, would she stay?

She turned to look at her little class working so diligently with the clay she had provided, a gift from Mrs. Salita. The children were very dear to her now. She would miss them when she left for home. Home! Would she go home and try to nurse Ernest Leigh back to health? What if Frank never came home? What if he had died in battle. What if he had just forgotten her?

I could stay. Minna surprised herself with the thought. *I could be happy here if not for Miss Pynchon who never seems happy with what I'm doing. Her, I wouldn't miss!*

"Remember the children must come first." She could hear Miss Pynchon's nasally voice chirping in her thoughts. *Back to work!*

Minna was further surprised when she stood at the schoolroom door as the children filed out, little Maria hugged her waist fiercely.

"Please don't go away Miss Minna!"

***

When every child had left the schoolroom proudly sporting a pinch pot or clay turtle, Robert came seeking another mission of mercy. He was of a mind to visit Leon's sister and the baby, and thought it seemly to have a woman with him for propriety's sake.

"I could ask Mrs. Salita if you prefer..."

Minna grabbed her clutch bag off the schoolroom table she used for a desk. "No, no. I would like to see Emma and the baby."

"I hear they have named the baby, Roland, after his father."

"Has there been any word from Roland?'

"He's safe the last they heard.."

Minna jerked the door open to the toodlelooka. *Thank you Lord!* "Law me, that family has suffered enough."

87

Minna looked out the open window as the toodlelooka ambled along the bumpy roads to Acomita. She was thinking about the old hound dog she had left at home when she moved out west to take this job. That old dog wasn't much to look at. She had at best questionable parentage, walked with a limp and stank to high heaven but there had never been another dog past or present that could equal her loyalty.

I am just like her, Minna thought. *I could never compete with the likes of Esmae Pynchon when it came to style and sophistication.* Is that what had happened to Frank? Perhaps he had met someone in the service that outranked her in such a way. He was maybe too kindhearted to tell her she just didn't measure up. Was that it? Best not to think of it. She mentally erased her disturbing thoughts.

Emma's place looked deserted but when Minna and Robert went to the door a relative met them with a scowl on her face.

Robert inquired after Emma and the woman blocking the doorway shook her head to every question.

"Maybe she doesn't speak English," Minna offered.

"Ga-wa-tse. Trooty gu-wa shruh? Hello, what is your name?"

The woman frowned and made shooing motions with her hands.

Just as they were about to give up, they heard Emma's soft voice within. "Who is it?"

"Emma, it's *Kenuty* and *Dyety*. We have come to see you and the baby, is it not a good time?"

Emma appeared in the doorway. She was holding the baby.

Minna couldn't believe how much the baby had grown already! It was pudgy and cherubic with little round cheeks.

"How precious!" Minna said out loud.

Emma giggled and handed the baby to her. The frowning relative stood aside and let them enter, clearly still not happy about it.

"This is my cousin, Lena." Emma said. "She doesn't speak English. Come in! Come in! Are you hungry?"

"*Hah, Da-wa-eh*! Yes, thank you, " Robert said. "I'm hungry. *Se-yu-mush-toow.*"

Emma twisted her lips in the direction of a table loaded with food.

"We have too much food. Please, help us eat it!"

Minna shifted baby Roland to the other arm. *Hope this child doesn't get stuck with the nickname, Roly-Poly when he's older!*

Robert wrapped a taco in a napkin. " We just wanted to see how you and the baby are getting along and see if you need anything."

"No, I don't need anything but thank you for all you have done. Gloria and Leon have been bringing groceries. Lena has been helping me with the baby."

"We are all hoping Roland will return to you soon." Minna said.

"*Hah,* we have word of a possible job for him when he gets back, with a logging company over to Turquoise Mountain."

"That's wonderful Emma!" Robert exclaimed.

Emma touched Minna's arm and took the baby back in hers.

"Would you like a word of prayer before we go?" Robert asked.

Emma looked back and forth between them and awkwardly at her cousin Lena.

"Um. Yes. I guess that would be all right."

Robert took Emma by the hand and laid his other hand on the baby's head.

"Dear Lord," he said. "We just ask for the blessings you have in mind for this family. Please give Roland a safe journey home. Bless and comfort Emma and help this child to continue to strengthen and enjoy good health. In Jesus' name we pray. Amen."

"Amen." Emma and Minna whispered together.

Robert and Minna hurried back to the toodlelooka and continued down the road back toward Laguna.

"I am glad to see the baby seems quite healthy," Minna said.

"Yes, and Emma seems in good spirits," Robert continued driving through Acoma reservation. He looked in his rear view mirror and noticed another car fast approaching.

"Unusual to see another car out here." he commented.

The other car quickly overtook the toodlelooka and as it passed the man driving yelled something that neither Robert nor Minna could understand.

"I think he wants you to stop," Minna said.

So Robert did.

The man did a U turn and drove back to where they had parked.

"Did you want to see me about something?" Robert said amiably.

"Yes, I certainly did." The man said, coming over to Robert's vehicle. "I want to know who gave you permission to come on this reservation?"

Robert's face registered surprise.

"Permission? I didn't know we required any special permission to come." he said. "Other than from the Lord, that is" he added.

"The Lord? But you've got to get permission from me."

"From you? Who are you, may I ask?"

The man looked at Robert scornfully. " I am the governor of Acoma."

"The governor? Well, we don't mean any disrespect. We were just visiting friends here."

"I've heard of you and we don't want you having any services here. We are all Catholics and we don't allow but one religion."

"I wasn't having services. Just visiting friends."

"Well, we don't want you here."

"We were just leaving."

"Good bye then."

"*Dru-we shots*, Good bye."

Robert tipped his hat and drove on.

Minna turned in her seat and looked back.

"Law me!" she whispered.

It was a hint of things to come.

***

Exactly one week later the governor of Laguna arrived on the schoolroom doorstep with the ceremonial Lincoln cane, symbol of his authority. There had been 13 canes delivered to each of the 13 pueblos as a sign of respect from Abraham Lincoln . These canes were highly treasured and still used in ceremonies. Robert and Minna were invited to attend. Invited. It felt more like "summoned" to Robert.

The folding chairs were quickly arranged in several concentric circles. The governing council sat in the centermost circle. Robert, Minna and Mrs. Salita sat in the outermost circle.

Robert tried not to appear nervous. He had appreciated the fact that the governor had not requested the room in any sort of intimidating way. He treated Robert and Minna in a friendly, cordial manner. Even so, it was apparent that the meeting was about them and whatever happened this day would definitely shape their futures on the Laguna reservation.

Minna was leaning forward in her chair, intent on every word. Robert could imagine how frightened she must be! He instinctively patted her hand and when she turned her eyes on him *those amazing blue eyes,* he smiled reassuringly.

Some of the council members spoke only in Keresan. Mrs. Salita translated in a whisper.

It was not good.

It was what they had heard before. The school was unnecessary, the nuns ran a school up the hill. There was no need of religious services in the schoolroom since they were all Catholics.

Everyone listened to the barrage of complaints, then the governor asked if there was anyone who wanted to say something on Robert's behalf.

Mrs. Salita was first in line.

"Not all of us are Catholic," she began. "Robert, *Kenuty*, has never said anything against that religion or any other. He has sometimes pointed out the differences in how he believes, but only as facts for us to know. He leaves how we believe up to us. That is all I have to say."

While Mrs. Salita was speaking Albert slipped in and took a seat next to Robert. When Minna smiled at him, he winked.

Leon was next. "I just want you to know what *Kenuty* has done for me and my family. First of all, he has helped my wife and me stop butting heads like a couple of rams out at sheep camp." Leon smiled warmly at Gloria who favored him with a radiant smile in return. "And speaking of sheep camp, *Kenuty* has never turned us down when we needed a ride out there. He has saved me personally many a day of hitchhiking. As for *Dyety*... she was willing, even at the risk of displeasing her boss lady, to go with Robert and me to bring Emma and the twins back from Albuquerque." There was much whispering as Leon paused. "I feel it is good for Laguna to have them both here. That is all I have to say." Leon sat down.

The governor asked if there was anyone else? Albert stood up.

"I just want to say no one could ask for a better friend than *Kenuty*," he paused. All heads turned to look at him. "..he is the best friend I ever had, dead or alive," he added.

Albert sat back down and the Governor said, "Robert, you have heard what everyone else has to say, do you wish to say anything?"

Robert stood up and cleared his throat. The governor nodded encouragingly.

"Well, I thank all of you who have had kind words to say about me. For those of you that are not happy with me being here, I am sorry if I have offended you in any way. I have tried the best I know how to be a friend to all of you. Albert, you must know that I am not the best friend you could have. I am able to be your friend because Jesus is my best friend and the best friend you could have too. I would hope that they would agree with me on that up the hill."

There was more whispering until the governor rapped his cane on the table. All became silent.

"Miss Cagle, *Dyety*, do you wish to say anything?"

Minna swallowed hard and slowly rose to her feet. "When I first came here I didn't know what to expect. I want to thank all of you that have been friendly to me and my work. I have become so very fond of your children who continue to teach me as much as I do them." She gazed around the room searching for friendly faces. Many smiled back. "I hope to stay," Minna said sincerely. "I hope to stay as long as you will allow me to."

Robert's heart leapt up in enthusiastic hopefulness.

***

Laguna
July 25

Dear Frank,

I am sending this to the last address I had for you and I hope and pray it finds you well and unharmed. You must be wondering about Ernest Leigh's situation. I don't know if you are aware he is home now with our parents. If you are able, I am sure it would do him a world of good to hear from you.

Frank, if you could just send me a note saying you are all right. I haven't heard from you in a very long time and of course I imagine the worst. Please let me know how you are doing. I miss you.

As ever,
Minna

NINE

Nop-sin-i-she ho-e-nyu-tra-nye dyu-ma she,
we shkui-ya-ni-shi nyukch go.
(Thou preparest a table before me in the presence of mine enemies.)

The council, the governor and his cane, and all the "witnesses" had left. The verdict was in.

Minna was to stay on as summer English teacher just as contracted. The council wanted the school used as a school and also wanted to stay in the good graces of the state officials. A public school would be available in the community.

Robert's situation was a little more precarious. Although the council agreed unanimously he could continue to live at the schoolhouse as long as he needed to, they now asked that he no longer hold religious services there.

"You may still hold services in the homes in which you are welcome," the governor had proclaimed. "..And *Kenuty*, let me be the first to invite you to my home for services this Sunday."

As the governor was leaving, he had a further invitation. "We are holding harvest dances at Seama on Thursday. You and *Dyety* should come."

Robert hesitated.

The governor chuckled. "I'm coming to one of your services, you come to one of ours."

***

Mrs. Salita smiled approvingly on the line of Eagle dancers stepping across the plaza. Their precision steps were so light that they scarcely left any footprints in the dust.

The singer greeted them with his high pitched song and the drummers beat louder and with more and more enthusiasm. The lead dancer blew his eagle bone whistle and the formation arced into a circle as the steps came faster. As the dancers swooped and soared, arms outstretched, wings and tail feathers swished past Mrs. Salita in a blur. Glancing upward, she sighed with satisfaction, noting where Minna and Robert sat on top of one of the flat-topped adobe houses. Minna's hair was tied in a scarf.

No tourist could tell her from the other native women. She's one of us!

After the disaster of the past few days, Mrs. Salita was having a glimmer of hope. She had observed how gently Robert assisted Minna up the ladder to their present perch, and how warmly Minna accepted his assistance!

Mrs. Salita concentrated on the dancers. Of all the traditional dances of the day, this was her favorite. Steeped in the history of her people she could almost physically see the people's prayers flying up to heaven carried by brother eagle.

The drummers gradually slowed the tempo until the dancers came to rest with wings folded and head bent downward. All left the plaza for a break and Mrs. Salita moved toward the wall below Minna and Robert.

"Come with me," she said. "I know where we can eat."

Robert assisted Minna in descending the ladder.

While they all sat at the kitchen table of a nearby neighbor, a teenage boy shyly approached them.

"Amos!" Mrs. Salita exclaimed.

The boy ducked his head and looked away, then slowly turned back toward Robert. He was holding something behind his back.

"*Ga-wa-tse*, Amos," Robert said. "What have you got there?"

Amos thrust a book toward Robert. The cover was singed at the edges. "I found this, *Kenuty*. It wasn't me that took it!"

Robert examined the damaged book. It was one of the translated hymnals that had been missing lo these many days.

Mrs. Salita grabbed the boy by the wrist. "Where did you find this? Show us!"

Amos led the way out of the house, down the dusty street beyond the main plaza, behind another row of houses, down a brush covered hill, into a trash filled ditch. Most of the trash had been burned to ashes. There was a pile of hymn books, not all had burned. Robert jumped into the ditch with an exclamation of happy surprise. "Some of these can still be used!"

***

Sunday, August 5

"How about page 242? Anybody have the full page?" Robert held his hymnal up to show the small group of people who had gathered for Sunday service at the governor of Laguna's house.

"I have it!" One of the young people cried. "Send *Da Light!*"

Minna flipped through the pages of the battered hymnal that she was holding.

"I have it too," she noted with glee. *This is just like bingo!*

***

Monday morning Minna had been waiting so long for Miss Pynchon to arrive from Albuquerque with her mail and weekly assessment that Robert must have felt obligated to offer a bite of lunch, blackberry jam and peanut butter crackers. Mrs. Salita had come over to see why Minna was so late coming in and she decided to eat a few crackers with them as well. She spent most of the meal complaining about the council's decision.

"What is the matter with those old prune faced coyotes?" she said. "Know what I think? I think they have sat around so long in the sun, their brains have gotten moldy!"

Minna put her cracker down, with a sudden loss of appetite.

"Sorry." Mrs. Salita frowned.

Robert continued eating. "They are the governing body," he said. "We have to abide by what they say."

There was a knock on the schoolroom door and they heard Miss Pynchon's voice. "Helloo."

"We're in here, " Minna called.

Miss Pynchon let herself into the schoolroom, her nylons swishing.

"Oh, you are eating. Sorry I'm late."

"Would you like some crackers?" Robert asked. "I seem to have an over-abundance of them."

Miss Pynchon crinkled her nose. "No, no. I can't stay long. I am so busy you know. I just came to see Marsha here this time."

"Minna." Minna said with her mouth full of cracker.

Mrs. Salita looked at Miss Pynchon suspiciously. "Another moldy brain," she said under her breath.

"Pardon?" Miss Pynchon inclined her head.

"I said, we are hoping for rain," Mrs. Salita said loudly.

"I came through a rainstorm on the way here from Albuquerque."

"What a blessing! I hope it finds us!" Robert stood up as if to leave.

Mrs. Salita almost forgot why she had come.

"Robert, I have news before you go." Mrs. Salita stood also and smoothed her dress.

"Good news, I hope."

Mrs. Salita smiled brightly. "Yes, good. It seems Gloria and Leon have patched things up. So much so in fact, they are talking of a wedding."

"A wedding?" Robert picked up his box of crackers and pushed his folding chair back into place the way Minna had them arranged for the children.

"*Hah.* You know the first time they were married according to the Laguna custom. Now they want to be married according to the laws of New Mexico. They have applied for the necessary license and they want you to officiate at their wedding."

"How wonderful!" Miss Pynchon jumped right into the conversation. "I just love weddings! Oh, do you think they would mind if I attended?"

***

The wedding was set for August 14th. In deference to the new council rules, it would have to be held in a home, not the schoolroom chapel. If Mrs. Salita had her way it would be held in the governor's house. It was larger than hers and would hold more of the family than her own place. The governor had not offered and Gloria had said it would be presumptuous to ask. Roland and Emma had a pretty place up at Acomita but that was a problem. Robert didn't feel welcome on the Acoma reservation and didn't want to stir things up.

Robert announced he would like to hold an outdoor wedding.

Mrs. Salita was astounded.

Where in the world would be appropriate for such a momentous occasion?

Mrs. Salita was proud of her house and her little garden which was mostly prickly cactus plants in the front of the house. It was shadier usually in the back where her horno oven sat but that "garden" was mostly weeds.

"I had in mind a nice place up on the mesa," Robert offered.

The mesa!

"How can we carry all that food up there?"

"I was thinking we could have the ceremony up on the mesa, then come down here and use the schoolroom for a reception. A reception isn't a religious service."

"No, it isn't. We eat food in there all the time don't we?"

"If anyone objects, we can bless the food outside and then come inside to eat it!"

***

Minna was happy for Gloria and Leon and Mrs. Salita, *bless her heart,* but she was not looking forward to this wedding herself.

For one thing Miss Pynchon was going to be there! She had pushed herself right into the plans. The family of the bride had agreed to have her come out of politeness, but Minna felt her teeth on edge every time she thought of it.

On the morning of the wedding Miss Pynchon arrived like a celebrity movie star.

She had piled her hair even higher on her head, applied cosmetics to almost clown proportions and was, Minna noticed, sporting an outrageous pair of expensive high heeled shoes.

Minna had to keep her smile from revealing what she was thinking, *Law me! I can't wait to see her try to climb the mesa in those things!*

"Mary!" Miss Pynchon exclaimed. "That dress, how precious!"

"Minna," she held her breath against the onslaught of Miss Pynchon's perfume.

Minna had chosen her outfit carefully, her best light weight belted dress with the tiny little raised polka dots. Now, in comparison to Miss Pynchon she felt like an attendant at the candy counter in Niota back home.

Miss Pynchon, as usual, was dressed to distraction! Her dress would be far fancier than the bride's! It was black, cinched at the waist with a large white sash, matching wide collar and huge white bow on one shoulder.

Minna found herself feeling vaguely depressed as she watched Miss Pynchon pull many packages out of her vehicle. Presents for the bride and groom. Minna had nothing to give them herself and no money to buy anything.

Gloria met them at the door to her mother's house. She was wearing a plain beige colored skirt and a white ruffled blouse. Her hair was pulled back with a white satin ribbon and Minna noticed Gloria had a new pair of white moccasin styled boots. *How sensible for climbing the mesa!* They were in stark contrast to Miss Pynchon's high heeled shoes.

"Gloria, you look lovely!" Minna exclaimed.

Gloria smiled shyly. "It's Leon's favorite." Gloria was holding the screen door open so Minna and Miss Pynchon entered the house. It was packed with relatives and friends. Minna spied Robert across the room. He had spiffied up as well. He was wearing crisp khaki pants and white shirt and bolo tie. He was clutching a black leather covered Bible to his chest.

As soon as it was determined everyone had arrived, the whole entourage set about climbing the mesa.

Minna forgot about being disgruntled and started to enjoy the climb. Twice she had to stop and pull pebbles from her shoe. Looking back, she could see that was nothing compared to the difficulties Miss Pynchon was having climbing in her high heels.

At last Miss Pynchon sat down on a rock, fanning herself. "I simply can't go any further," she moaned.

Those closest to her looked on with amused sympathy. Finally, a couple of young men lifted a sputtering Miss Pynchon up and took turns carrying her the rest of the way. Her red face eventually accepted the attention and settled into a self satisfied smile. Minna secretly rolled her eyes at the spectacle.

There was a nice breeze up there on the mesa and the view was dramatic, as always. Minna found herself day dreaming. Could it be like this at her own wedding? She would love for Frank to see this! She agreed with Robert, there couldn't be a lovelier place to make vows to each other, to God, to His creation. And what better person to tie the knot but her friend Robert?

She gazed on him fondly. She would miss him when she left this place. She would miss this place! The friends she had made, the children, even those silly bats in the cave.

"For this cause shall a man leave his father and mother, and shall be joined unto his wife, and they two shall be one flesh," Robert read. "This is the great mystery: but I speak concerning Christ and the Church. Nevertheless let everyone of you in particular so love his wife even as himself; and the wife see that she reverence her husband."

I have reverenced Frank! But has he loved me even as himself? Minna's shoulders drooped. She didn't think so. Not if he is alive and well…

The "I do's" exchanged, the group started back down off the mesa. There was much laughter and well wishes following the happy couple!

Robert was assisting in the toting of Miss Pynchon. Minna noted how flushed his face was as he carefully descended the rocky path. *Oh, my! Hope he isn't about to have a heart attack!*

They were nearly all the way back to the schoolroom when an enormous racket started up in the village. A few cars and pick up trucks were circling through the village, horns blaring. Some people were even gathered beside Robert's toodlelooka pushing on the horn.

At first Minna thought it was in honor of the wedding, a local custom perhaps. But No! Some children came squealing toward them.

"It's over! It's over!"

Minna looked at the bride and groom. They seemed as confused as she.

Some older boys skipped passed yelling, "The war! The war is over! We heard it on the radio at McCarty's trading post."

Robert could not stop laughing. *The war is over!* How he had prayed for peace! He could not even sort his thoughts out. *Exhilaration to the point of flabbergastation!*

He did not even mind the very silly Miss Pynchon who was jumping up and down like a schoolgirl.

"I'm going to Paris!" She was chirping. "Daddy told me before he died that I should see Paris with his inheritance money when this war is over!"

"I'm happy for you." Robert said sincerely. "I'm happy for everyone!"

Indeed everyone seemed to be celebrating. Many hugs. Some tears. Much hand pumping. It truly was a wonderful time to celebrate the wedding.

Robert looked for Minna. Now her young man would be coming back to claim her, he supposed. A sobering thought. He glanced over the exuberant crowd for that polka dot dress and could find no sign of it. Where had she gone?

Minna sat down on her bed and tried to settle her breathing. She had trouble deciding if it was elation she felt or dread.

She hadn't seen or heard from Frank in seven months. Was he alive or dead? One thing for sure, now that the war was over, she would be finding the answer to that question soon.

She held his photograph in her trembling hand and tried not to think of another possibility.

Maybe he just doesn't care for me anymore.

She closed her tear filled eyes and whispered, "Lord, help me to know the truth. Help me to know what to do with the truth. I am trusting you to see me through this."

Minna felt a sense of gentle peace descending on her. How surprising! *There may be something to this prayer business.*

Minna stood up purposefully and returned Frank's photo to the dresser. She set her lips in a firm straight line. *I can go celebrate with the others now. It's in God's hands!*

Mrs. Salita sat down with a plop next to Robert. She noticed his heaped up plate of food and sighed with contentment. *He hasn't found a wife yet, but he won't find any cooking better than this!* Mrs. Salita's thoughts turned to her own son who had not survived the war. *The war is over, that is good. If only it had ended before it took my Robby.* She let her gaze fall on Robert again. *How like my son he is! Robby so enjoyed my cooking. He had the same tenderhearted nature, the same sense of humor…*

"Have you seen Minna?" Robert asked. "Where do you suppose she has got to?"

Probably the outhouse. "Somewhere important I'm sure. She wouldn't be missing this, Robert." *Minna likes my cooking too!*

They both scanned the crowd. Mrs. Salita smiled at Gloria and Leon. She surprised herself with the warm feelings she now had for that Acoma boy!

"There she is!" they both said at once.

Minna was taking the baby out of Emma's arms. They were both laughing.

Minna cuddled the baby up next to her cheek and walked over to join Mrs. Salita and Robert. She had barely sat down next to Robert when Miss Pynchon sashayed up.

"Oh, Matilda! Wonder if you'd mind moving my auto? I'll hold the baby." She proffered the keys and shook them until they jingled.

Now what is she up to? Mrs. Salita cast a suspicious eye on Miss Pynchon. It was quite evident where Miss Pynchon's eye was cast. *Oh no you don't!*

Mrs. Salita snatched the dangling keys out of Miss Pynchon's hand as she popped up out of her seat.

"I'll take care of it," she announced and was gone before Miss Pynchon realized what had happened. *She just wants to dispose of Minna so she can sit next to Robert! Hmmpfh! We'll see about that!*

Mrs. Salita strode toward Miss Pynchon's vehicle purposefully. After all, how hard could it be? She had seen Robert operate the toodlelooka hundreds of times. She looked at the keys in her hand critically. Well, she had no need of these. She had no intention of actually turning this contraption on. That simplified things. Then she only needed the wheel and the brake!

"You," she indicated one of the boys playing outside the schoolhouse, "...and you," she included his friend. "Come with me."

The boys followed her to the vehicle and then at her behest pushed it backward while she turned the steering wheel.

Having relocated the vehicle behind the school house, Mrs. Salita smiled with satisfaction. She took a moment to admire the interior of Miss Pynchon's car. She knew the boys were laughing at her, but she didn't care. Laboriously, she rolled down the window.

"*Da-wa-eh!* Thank you!"

Mrs. Salita unlatched the door and trudged back up the hill to the schoolroom feeling very pleased with herself. She was examining a new idea she was formulating when she returned to the schoolroom. *Oh my! I kept her from taking Dyety's seat and gave her mine!* There sat Robert between Minna and Miss Pynchon. He was leaning toward Miss Pynchon politely listening to whatever foolishness she had come up with now.

"Robert, could I speak with you?" Mrs. Salita said.

"Er, yes?" He looked up but made no move to get up..

"Outside?" Mrs. Salita insisted.

"All right." Robert stood and placed his plate of food on the chair.

"Yes?" He asked her once they had cleared the building.

"Robert, if you have time tomorrow, would you teach me how to drive? Oh, and I'm sure Minna would like to come too."

TEN

Se-mush-ka dye a-siaty' dyu-ia-un-yi.
(Thou anointest my head with oil.)

How did Mrs. Salita get me into this? Minna peered out the windshield at the stretch of winding road below.

"Are you sure you want me to start here?" she asked Robert.

"Yes. I want you to feel comfortable with the brake before anything else."

Minna glanced in the rearview mirror at Mrs. Salita in the middle of the back seat. She was huddled into herself with her arms crossed over her chest. *Hmph. I'm scaring her. Good. Serves her right for insisting I do this.* It was supposed to have been Mrs. Salita's driving lesson, but after insisting that Minna come along, Mrs. Salita had begged her to go first!

Driving wasn't totally foreign to Minna. She had attempted to drive the family farm truck with Ernest Leigh before the war. But she found it too challenging in front of her teasing brother and gave up, saying what did she need to drive for? She couldn't imagine ever owning a vehicle of her own.

Minna slowly lifted her foot off the brake and leaned into the first turn.

"Try to relax, Minna." Robert said helpfully.

Easy for you to say! Minna realized she was leaning as far forward as she could and gripping the steering wheel so hard, her hands hurt.

"You are doing fine. Try to lean back a little."

"I think I feel better where I am!" *Even if I do have to look through the steering wheel instead of over it!*

One more turn and then another. *Well, maybe this isn't too bad...*

"Remember to breathe," Robert said gently.

Oh! Minna released her breath as they neared the bottom of the hill. The toodlelooka began jerking on the straighter road.

"Now change gears like this, then slowly release your left foot." Robert placed his hand over hers on the gear shift. Minna was surprised to feel so comforted by it.

"Eh-hiay!" Mrs. Salita gasped as they went over an enormous bump. Minna instinctively braked and the automobile stalled out.

"Did I hit something?"

"I don't think so." Robert opened his door and leaned out to inspect the road. "Nope. Nothing I can see. Must have been one of those invisible deer."

"Invisible deer?"

"Yes, we'll know that's what it was if we see one on the side of the road when we come back."

"Ha!" Minna was not amused.

They started up again and Robert continued his coaching. At least this part of the road was relatively straight.

Uh, oh! Car up ahead. Minna threw the brake on again and the toodlelooka obliged by stalling out.

"Okay, let's try this again." Robert shifted over her hand again. She noted it was trembling. It could have something to do with the fact they were stalled on a railroad track!

Mrs. Salita lifted up in her seat and strained to see down the track.

"A train is coming!" she shrieked.

Robert kept his voice steady. "Clutch in Minna. Give it some gas."

They darted forward just as they heard the whistle.

Law me!

The road straightened out as they continued on, but there was a ditch to either side. Minna felt the safest place to be was right down the middle of the road. This would have worked beautifully had it not been for the car coming straight at them! She swerved and Robert sucked in his breath as they jumped the ditch and ran into the fence on the other side.

All were silent for a moment.

"Are you okay Mrs. Salita?" Minna turned to look at her. Mrs. Salita was hugging herself tightly but her body shook violently.

"Yes, *Dyety*. I'm okay," she said in a small voice. "Just cold," she added.

***

Robert jumped out of the vehicle and surveyed the damage. One thing was for sure, they would not easily rescue the toodlelooka from where it had come to rest. Going backward was out of the question because of the ditch. Going forward would be a problem also because of the sand. Sand was even worse than mud if you were stuck in it. And they were. Stuck.

Minna's mouth was closed in a tight straight line but her eyes were big as saucers.

"Are you both okay?" Robert asked. They both nodded vigorously.

"I am going to jog up there to that gas station and see if we can get some help."

It wasn't far but when Robert got there it became apparent that it was closed. Long closed. He doubted it had been used in years. He looked in at the dusty window. Empty. Now what?

There was an adobe house at some distance and nowhere else to find help, so he trudged onward. Luckily someone was home.

"Beg pardon," he said. "I'm *afred* we have had a little mishap up the road here. Do you have any equipment that could pull us out?"

The man at the door stepped outside and looked up the road to where they were stuck fast.

"Stuck in the sand, eh?"

"Yes."

"Who's going to fix my broken fence?"

107

"Er...that would be me."

"All right then." The man indicated the shed at the back of the house and Robert was relieved to see an old tractor that apparently still worked.

Minna and Mrs. Salita stood on the side of the road while the man attached a chain from the tractor to the car. The wheels spun in place and the toodleooka groaned as if in pain. Robert looked the other way. *What a mess!*

Something about the abandoned gas station perked his interest. Good sized building. Almost as big as the schoolhouse. *Hmmm. I wonder…*

At last the earth gave up her prisoner and the car pulled free of the sand. The helpful neighbor took it all the way to the crossroads and Robert hastened to catch up with him. At last they both stopped and the gentleman jumped down to detach the car from the tractor. Robert inspected the vehicle and saw no damage other than some severe scratches on the front bumper where it had hit the fence. The fence was in far worse shape.

"I will get some lumber and some tools and come by tomorrow to repair your fence Mr. ah…"

"Stevens. Bud Stevens." The man extended his hand and Robert grasped it.

"I'm Robert Carlisle. I am so sorry for the inconvenience. Do you have some animal stock in danger of escape?"

"Just a few goats. I'll pen 'em up until you can get the job done. Appreciate your seeing to it as soon as possible."

"Of course. Of course. I'll get right on it." Robert's gaze returned to the adobe gas station. "I wonder Mr. Stevens, do you happen to know who owns the abandoned gas station yonder?"

"I certainly do. That would be me. You lookin' to open a gas station? I can give you a good price but I must in all honesty warn you, not much traffic comes by here in Cubero."

"I have something else in mind. We'll talk about it when I come tomorrow."

***

"'Preciate you coming out here with me, Albert." Robert grasped the other end of the plank they were hauling out of the toodlelooka."

"*We-meh*, that's all right. I just wanted to see what a preacher says when he hits his thumb with a hammer." Albert's eyes twinkled.

Robert paused to consider. "*An-yu-me-dze ha-ma-ha,*" he said. "Good story." Robert thought about his morning so far as they worked. He had been all the way to Albuquerque and back picking up lumber, visiting the mission board office and delivering the card to the post office that Minna had asked him to mail for her.

He felt a little guilty about that card. His curiosity had gotten the better of him. Now he was disturbed by what it said. Minna had written to her brother pleading with him to send word about Frank. Robert didn't know what to make of it. Was this fellow dead, missing or unbelievably crass in casting her off? Robert swung the hammer unnecessarily hard at the thought.

"Looks like I'll know the answer to my story soon." Albert mused.

"Well, my friend. We'll have this job done in no time." Robert banged on another plank and tested its strength with a kick.

"So why isn't *Dyety* out here helping you repair this fence?"

"She has lessons this morning and she feels bad enough. Thought I'd get the job done quietly and not embarrass her any further. Besides..." Robert said glancing at the abandoned gas station down the road. "I'm on a mission for the mission."

Albert pushed his cowboy hat back off his forehead and followed Robert's gaze to its source.

"You thinking of moving out here?"

"I'm authorized to look it over and make an offer if it will be suitable."

Albert's face fell.

"You won't be living at Laguna any more?"

***

109

Mrs. Salita dried her hands on a dish towel as she looked out her kitchen window.

What does that old Tom cat want now? Hmmph. Might as well offer him some coffee.

She opened her front door and beckoned Albert in. He seemed anxious.

"*Ga-wa-tze,* Albert," Mrs. Salita said.

"*Ga-wa-tze.* I was hoping you were home."

"Come in and have some coffee."

"*Hah.* That would be good." Albert followed her into the kitchen and took a seat at the kitchen table. Mrs. Salita noticed from the corner of her eye that he sat up straight with both feet on the floor. He put his old battered hat on his lap. Albert said nothing while she reheated the morning's coffee but when she sat a steaming mug in front of him and slid the sugar bowl over he began speaking in an uncharacteristically excited manner.

"We've got to do something I am thinking. We are about to see Robert move out of the schoolhouse. It is all because he has found a place over to Cubero. He thinks he can have services there and live in the back of the building." Albert looked over his shoulder and said in a whisper, "And did you know *Dyety* has a soldier sweetheart?"

"She's at the schoolhouse. She can't hear you." Mrs. Salita sat down heavily across the table from Albert.

"A sweetheart you say?"

"Yes, apparently she has been trying to get word on where he is since the war is over."

"You think he may have been killed?"

"Could be. I think Robert is conflicted in his feelings about her."

"We can't wait to find out about some distant sweetheart. She could be leaving before that works out."

"Well, now that he is moving, how are we going to get them together?"

"Leave that to me."

***

Minna watched as the last of her students skipped across the road outside the schoolhouse. A smile played at her lips. She sat down and placed a clean sheet of paper in front of her. Picking up her fountain pen she touched her nose as she thought of what to write.

Laguna
August 17

Dear Sissy,

Did I tell you what my Laguna nick-name has become? Wee rabbit wiggle nose! "Dyety" for short which just means "rabbit". I have been thinking a lot about my experiences over the summer and as I think about coming home I am both glad and sad. I miss all of you of course and I have so much to tell you that I couldn't begin to write it all in a letter. How I shall miss these children! And yes, Sissy, I have discovered some very cute boys in New Mexico. They are five, six and seven years old!

I must tell you seriously though, Sissy, when it comes to boys, being cute doesn't amount to a hill of beans! Why, even Winston Churchill was a handsome young man once and now look at him!

Minna thought of how Frank had not written to her. Not even once!

And sometimes the ones you think you know best do some very unexpected things...

"*Dyety!*" She heard Albert as he hastened from the direction of Mrs. Salita's house. He was carrying a large picnic basket. Minna's eyes crinkled with amusement. She stuffed her letter back in her notebook.

"I see you have brought a little snack," she said.

"*Hah.* Is Robert here?"

"Yes. I believe so." She called over her shoulder, "Robert?"

"Is that from Mrs. Salita?" Minna asked.

"*Hah.* She made too much food, she said you and Robert should take it up on the mesa for a picnic."

Robert came from behind his privacy curtain with a towel around his neck. He was half shaved. "How nice! Won't you join us Albert?"

Albert's face fell. "Oh. No, no. I have already eaten. You two go ahead. It would be a shame to see all this food go to waste."

Robert and Minna glanced at each other.

"I'll get my scarf." Minna said.

***

Robert was mentally beating himself up. He fully realized this was probably his last chance to declare himself to Minna. *I've got to say something!*

"Er, you know Minna, I'll be moving out of the schoolhouse soon."

Minna put down her cup of lemonade. "No, I didn't know. Where will you go Robert?"

Robert rearranged his legs on the blanket and straightened his back.

"Well, you know that day you were driving the first time?"

"Yes, how could I forget?"

"Well, the fellow that owns that property also owns the abandoned gas station just down the road from there at Cubero. The mission board has authorized me to purchase the property. It is big enough to hold services in the front of the building and it is already set up with a kitchen space and a couple of rooms in the back."

"Electricity?"

"Yes! And running water!"

"That's wonderful Robert! I am happy for you. We will miss you at the schoolhouse though. Guess I'll be leaving soon too."

This is it! It is now or never...

Robert stood up nervously and shook the kinks out of his legs. He turned his back so Minna couldn't see how deeply he was blushing. She couldn't see his face.

112

"I'm not sure I could let you leave, Minna, without telling you how I feel…" he began. While he was searching for the right words Minna said, "You will have to write to me when I go back home to Tennessee and tell me how it all works out."

"Um, yes. I was hoping I could persuade you to stay, Minna…" Robert turned to face her. She was looking off in the distance. She didn't respond!

Robert leaned over and whispered in Minna's ear, "..because I love you," he whispered. He whispered in her left ear.

Minna turned toward him, an expectant smile on her face but said nothing.

Robert waited for a response but receiving none he began to put things back in the picnic basket.

"Guess we better be getting back," he said, crestfallen.

"Oh. All right." Minna helped him repack the basket and they set off arduously climbing back down toward the village. Robert struggled to keep his emotions in check. He was in for an even worse shock.

There was a young man in uniform at Mrs. Salita's door. He was leaning on a cane and Mrs. Salita looked worried.

Minna gasped, then began running to the young man. They embraced exuberantly.

Robert couldn't believe the timing. *Look at that, Frank has finally come for her!*

Robert slipped into the schoolhouse without even waiting to be introduced.

***

"Ernest Leigh! Why didn't you tell me you were coming? We would have met you in Santa Fe. How did you get here?"

"By bus. And I hitchhiked some." Ernest Leigh held Minna at arms' length. "You look good, Minner. I thought you might be skinny as a rail or something."

"Mrs. Salita keeps me well fed. Oh. I'm sorry…" Minna realized Mrs. Salita was still standing in her door. "Mrs. Salita, this is my brother Ernest Leigh come all the way from Tennessee. Ernest Leigh, this is my landlady and friend, Mrs. Salita."

Ernest Leigh held out his hand and Mrs. Salita squeezed it.

"Won't you come in out of the hot sun?" she said.

"Thank you, Ma'am. I could sit a spell, I reckon."

Minna wrapped an arm around his waist. He picked up a satchel and they all went inside.

"I'll make some coffee." Mrs. Salita disappeared into her kitchen. Minna showed Ernest Leigh to a chair in the main room of the house.

"I got your letter the same day as I heard from a navy buddy, lives in California. He thinks he can get me a job of work there if I come out right away. So, I thought I might as well swing by to see you on the way."

"Oh, Ernest Leigh! It is so good to see you!" Minna brushed a tear away before he could see it.

"Well, I'm not much to look at these days." Ernest Leigh indicated his leg with his cane. "I look a great deal like our *aint* Ivy, don't you think?"

"You look wonderful to me, Ernest Leigh." Minna said sincerely.

Mrs. Salita arrived with the coffee, took one look at Ernest Leigh's serious face and excused herself from the room claiming she had a wash load on the line and had to get it inside before it collected too much dust. "I'm sure you two need to catch up," she noted.

Ernest Leigh broke the silence after she left.

"I want to thank you Minner, for sending the youngun's stories my way. You can't imagine how much they cheered me in my hour of need."

"They cheer me as well. They have become very precious to me," Minna replied.

Ernest Leigh opened the satchel he had brought. Stirring inside it he chose a few pieces of paper and handed them to Minna.

"Ernest Leigh! You didn't have to bring the stories back." She tried to push them back at him but he held up his hands, shaking his head.

"No, no. You don't understand. Turn them over."

Minna did so. There were pencil drawings on the back. Humorous cartoons. Ernest Leigh had illustrated the stories. Minna's face brightened with understanding.

"These are wonderful!"

Ernest Leigh had a lop-sided grin. "Thought your students might enjoy them, since they shared their stories with me."

Minna knew Ernest Leigh was trying to get around to telling her about Frank. She braced herself. *Is he dead? Please don't say he is dead!*

"Minner. I'm afraid I have some news that won't sit well…"

ELEVEN

So-wiash-ta-nyi ma-me go-wiami tsuh
(My Cup Runneth Over)

Robert grabbed his clothes off the curtain and threw them on the bed. *Might as well move out right now!* He pulled out a suitcase from under the bed, opened it and threw the clothes in unfolded. His shaving equipment went in and lastly his Bible.

Well, Lord, guess it is pretty clear you have other plans for Miss Minerva Cagle. Plans that don't include me! Robert rushed determinedly out the door and threw the suitcase in the trunk of his automobile. It took a few tries but he finally got the toodlelooka started and without looking back, he drove off in a cloud of dust.

***

"It's about Frank isn't it?" Minna found herself clutching the arm of the stuffed sofa. Clutching so hard her knuckles were white.

Ernest Leigh cleared his throat. He stared at the floor. Anywhere but at Minna.

"I would have let you know sooner Minner, if I had not been so deep into myself, so to speak." Ernest Leigh loosened his shirt and mopped his forehead with a handkerchief.

"You see, Frank was wounded also, but not at the same time as me. It was hard to find out when or where…"

Minna blinked back forming tears. "Go, on…"

"So, it turns out he has been in the hospital in the Philippines all this time."

"He's alive!" Minna closed her eyes and let out the breath she had been holding in.

"Yes, yes. He's alive…" Ernest Leigh stood up and moved over to the sofa where Minna was sitting. He sat down beside her and put an arm around her shoulders.

"He's alive Minner, but I'm sorry, seems he has got married."

"What?" Minna turned her good ear toward Ernest Leigh. "Did you say married?"

"Yes."

"Married?'

"Yes."

"But no! That's not possible. I don't understand."

Ernest Leigh took Minna's hand in both of his. "I know. I know. It was a shock to me too. You see, there was a nurse that took care of him in the hospital and well, they fell in love, I reckon. He is feeling bad he didn't tell you. Said he tried to write several times and just couldn't find the words."

"Couldn't find the words…" Minna repeated. She opened her mouth but found herself in the same difficulty.

"I'm sorry, Minner. I know you were sweet on him."

Minna saw the hurt look on Ernest Leigh's face and her heart melted for him. Ernest Leigh had been through so much and now had this awful duty. What a coward Frank was! Came all the way through a war and was too scared to face her with the truth!

"Why Ernest Leigh," she said as sweetly as she could manage under the circumstances. "…all this time I was sure he was dead. This is better news."

Or bitter news is more like it. Law me!

"You're okay with it?" Ernest Leigh asked in surprise.

"Of course I'm okay. I'm just surprised is all. He should have let me know, like you said." Minna said pragmatically. She hoped Ernest Leigh believed her. She would collapse later. Not in front of her brother. Her brave brother! She would be brave too. For now!

"I am glad you are taking it so well." Ernest Leigh continued. "I wanted to deliver the news in person. Not just some letter…and you know, it was on the way. More or less…"

"What are your plans? Can you stay? There are so many friends here I would like you to meet."

"Oh, can't stay. I am catching the 4:30 bus out of Grants. I need to get on the highway where maybe I can hitch a ride that much further."

"So soon? Maybe Robert could give you a ride to Grants."

"Robert's taken a load to Cubero." Mrs. Salita's voice came from the kitchen.

"I'm sorry." Her face appeared through the door. "Didn't mean to listen. But don't worry. I'll scare up my son-in-law. He can borrow the Sanchez truck and take you to Grants."

"I'll come too." Minna said.

"No, there's no need to put you out. We can say our good byes here."

"But you just got here!"

"Just passin' through Minner. I need to be on my way, now that I know you will be all right."

"I'll be all right."

***

Liar! Liar! Liar! Minna didn't know who she meant exactly. Herself, for telling Ernest Leigh she would be all right or Frank for never hinting this was happening. Married! How could he do this? And to think this was the reason for the lack of response to all her letters! Had he planned to just ignore her out of the way?

All this time I thought I loved him and now I feel like I hate him! Oh, if only Robert were here! Where is he? Why did he think he had to move out of the schoolroom so suddenly?

Minna knew Robert of all people would be able to comfort her. Hadn't he done so previously? She remembered crying in his arms the day they brought Emma's babies home from Albuquerque. How warm and how gentle his embrace had been. She thought about the way he had shown her the special place up on the mesa and how that had calmed her down. How pleasant the picnic was this morning…

Minna slipped out of Mrs. Salita's house and began pacing around the schoolhouse. If only Robert were here! How she needed a friend right now! Right now Robert seemed like her only friend. Her best friend! Minna remembered Albert's words the day they were all summoned to the council meeting. "He is the best friend anyone could have…" Then Robert had refuted that to say "Jesus is the best friend you could have."

Oh, Jesus! Be my friend now! I don't know what to do! Should I go home? The school board hasn't asked me to stay past the summer. How will I leave my friends here and go home to no prospects of a job? I had put all my hopes in Frank!

Minna picked up a pebble and threw it forcefully at the schoolhouse wall. *Take that Frank! Wish I could throw it at you! I was so wrong! I only had a schoolgirl crush…just like my silly little sister. I could never have made a life with Frank. It was all fantasy. I needed someone dependable. Someone…like…*

Someone like Robert!

Could Robert care for her? How could she know for sure? Could she live like this here among these people as his wife? Yes, she could! She wanted to stay!

***

"Wait for *Dyety*, she's coming too." Mrs. Salita climbed into the front seat of the toodlelooka. The back was full with Mrs. Leeds and her three children.

"Hit the horn!" All three children cried.

Robert smiled softly and pushed on the horn.

Ooooh-ooga!

The children squealed in delight.

Minna limped out of Mrs. Salita's front door, pulling on her shoe as she came.

"Mr. Robert! Let her drive!" The children begged.

Uh, oh! Didn't see this coming. Mrs. Salita squirmed in the front seat.

"Please! Pleeeeease!"

Robert laughed. "We will see what she says."

Minna gave the children a cross-eyed look as she approached the car. They screamed with laughter. "Come on Miss Minna. You drive!"

Mrs. Salita mopped her forehead with her handkerchief but said nothing. She knew the children were begging Minna to drive because with her uncertainty and inexperience it added an element of thrill each time she swerved or the automobile jerked and made grinding noises.

Minna sighed and took the driver's seat.

Eh-hiay!

It was worth it to Mrs. Salita to have Robert squeezed in between her and Minna on the front seat. She glanced approvingly each time he placed his hand over Minna's to help her find the proper gear position. Mrs. Salita knew this could very well be the last Sunday Minna would see Robert. The time was fast approaching when her summer job would be over and she could be going home! As far as she could tell her picnic scheme hadn't produced any fruit. Maybe Robert didn't know about that other fellow practically leaving Minna at the altar.

At the altar! Well, now. At the altar was a very good place for Dyety to be, seeing as she was likely to run into a certain young minister there!

***

Minna observed the new building with awe. She could understand Robert's attraction to the place. The front room was large enough for the usual size crowd that attended the services. Folks seemed to have no objection to standing for now. Robert had borrowed a few chairs from the schoolroom for the older folks.

Minna kept shifting from one foot to the other, peeking around congregant shoulders. How handsome Robert looked this morning! The blue shirt he was wearing brought out the clear blue New Mexico sky in his eyes! She scolded herself for not paying attention to what he was saying. After the last prayer, Robert invited all those that would like to see the rest of the building to tour it with him. Minna was eager to see.

Just behind the front room was a small kitchen. There was a camp stove set up there, a gift from one of the friends from Laguna. The windows were a bit grimy but the floor had been thoroughly swept. Down the hall were two sizeable rooms. Robert had put his iron bed and a chest of drawers in one of them. It was certainly better accommodations than where he had been at Laguna. It looked lonely, Minna thought. *He really needs a wife!* Minna blushed at the thought.

"…and my sister has made and sent me this." Robert indicated a braided rug on the floor beside his bed. "She calls it an accent rug."

"Accident rug?" Minna asked.

"Accent…accent rug."

Everyone laughed.

Law me!

After the tour it took Robert eight trips to take everyone home that needed a ride. For some reason Mrs. Salita kept motioning everyone else ahead of her. At last only Mrs. Salita and Minna were left. They decided to wait just outside the new mission door. Mrs. Salita looked upward at the roof of the porch.

"I don't like the looks of this porch," she declared. She whacked one of the beams with her walking stick. "Robert should see about taking this porch off altogether. It seems rotten to me."

"It may be unstable, perhaps we should wait for Robert over there under the tree." Minna and Mrs. Salita picked their way carefully to the shade. Mrs. Salita sat down heavily on a stump. She watched Minna's approach, started to speak, then stopped as if thinking better of it. She waited for Minna to catch up and join her in the shade.

"*Dyety*, I have been thinking about the last council meeting."

"Yes. I have too."

Mrs. Salita turned an intense gaze on her. "Did you really mean what you said, about staying here as long as we want you?"

Minna met Mrs. Salita's gaze with a sincere one of her own. "Yes. I mean that now more than ever."

121

Mrs. Salita's eyes widened. She gave a satisfied grunt. "Then I intend to do everything I can to make that happen!" For emphasis she stood up and thumped her walking stick firmly on the ground. "Now, where has that Robert got to? I need a ride over to the governor's house!"

***

Mrs. Salita spoke to Robert through the driver's side window.

"You take *Dyety* on home. I might be here awhile and I can walk home from here." *I'll walk all the way to Albuquerque if I have to...if it will get Minna to stay and you to marry her!* Mrs. Salita watched the toodlelooka pull away. Minna was looking puzzled out the passenger side window. *That's all right child, I'll take it from here!*

"*Ga-wa-tse!*" She hollered at the door.

The governor came to answer.

***

Robert blew out a sigh of frustration. How he longed to beg Minna to stay! To join him at Cubero and never leave! He could imagine a life together here in New Mexico with her and no other! She had not mentioned Frank but he knew her intentions were to return home and marry him.

Why must I suffer through this, Lord? Haven't I tried to stay out of their way? Out of the picture? I need your strength to get through this.

"When do you finish your obligations here for the summer, Minna?"

"I guess Miss Pynchon will tell me when she comes this Tuesday."

"This Tuesday? Ah...About Miss Pynchon..."

She looked up at him. Her eyes were glistening. *Those amazing eyes!*

122

"Minna, it shames me to say this, but I have no desire to see Miss Pynchon on Tuesday. She is under some…er…confusion concerning me and I think it best if I stay out at Cubero that day."

"Yes. I understand. Miss Pynchon is…" Minna grasped at words. Robert finished her thought for her.

"I think she is used to getting everything she wants. In any case, I would like to know how long you will be with us. Can you get word to me somehow?"

***

Minna watched the automobile disappear in a cloud of dust.

That's it then. For a moment I thought…well, I was wrong. I don't have Frank. I don't have Robert. ..

Minna went inside Mrs. Salita's and after changing out of her Sunday clothes, she left a note on the kitchen table. "*Mrs. Salita, I am going up on the mesa to think.*" Minna hurried on through the village, stopping once to look back at the house.

She knew what she wanted to see one last time. The cave! It seemed urgent for some reason. She climbed hand over hand up the mesa wall stopping only once more to pick a pebble out of her shoe. The whole sole was practically gone now and she was almost out of the cardboard she had been using to extend its life. She didn't drop the pebble but used it when she reached the cave to test for bats.

No bats today! Too bad! Could use a laugh.

The sunlight highlighted the ancient hand print on the wall of the cave. She thought about Robert again and what he had said about prayers and desires of the heart the day she had first seen that petroglyph.

There had been a rare rainstorm the night before and a single red clay mud puddle remained just outside the cave. Minna plunged her left hand in the mud and placed it carefully on the wall just below the petroglyph.

She surveyed the picture she had made. *Guess I have left my mark on New Mexico…*

Minna started to leave but hastened back to her mud painting. With her other hand she scratched a line across the ring finger.

She didn't see the young man setting his prayer stick up on the mesa, but he observed her as she descended the rocky path back to Laguna. It was Amos.

After she was completely out of view he climbed up the hill and bent over to look inside the bat cave. When he saw the muddy hand print she had left, he retreated leaving it undisturbed.

***

Tuesday, August 21st

Mrs. Salita heard the governor calling outside her front door.

"Ga-wa-tse!"

She dried her hands on a dish towel and hastened to answer. *"Ga-wa-tse!* Did you speak with Miss Pynchon?"

"I did."

Mrs. Salita opened the door wide. "Come in."

He did so.

"Well?"

"I told her we would like *Dyety* to stay but she said the school board has been considering someone else. She said she would tell them of our wishes but ultimately it is their decision since they will be the ones paying the salary."

"But they might consider it?"

"They might."

Mrs. Salita released her breath between her teeth. "When will we know?"

"When Miss Pynchon comes back next week. She will either have the news we are hoping for, or come to take *Dyety* back to the Santa Fe train station herself."

I can't let that happen!

TWELVE

She giatr-dye-mi da-wa-dze-e-she e iah-ya-wa dye ty-ia-se-pshro
yu-we nu-dah-go ha-maty se-u-shto he-mah
(Surely goodness and mercy will follow me all the days of my life)

Little Lucy Pedro placed an egg shaped rock on Minna's table.

"*Da-wa-eh*. Thank you, Lucy," Minna said. Her eyes were smiling but her heart was not.

The next child approached with a small woven dream catcher.

"*Da-wa-eh*, Audrey."

She heard an automobile approaching. Minna glanced anxiously out the schoolroom window. Her face fell. She had hoped to see the toodlelooka. But no.
It was Miss Pynchon's Cadillac convertible.

"*Da-wa-eh*, Henry." Minna said absent mindedly to the little boy with a pinch pot.

Minna could see out the window that Miss Pynchon was struggling with a large box.

"Excuse me for a moment children." Minna exited the building. "Need some help?" she asked Miss Pynchon.

"Oh, Mavis! Good! I have some things to give the children and then we can be on our way. I hope you have packed because I booked your train out of Santa Fe for 12:00 noon."

Law me! She can't wait to be rid of me!

"It's Minna."

"What?"

"Nothing." Minna took the other side of the box and they carried it into the schoolroom. Two giggling children sat up straight in their chairs as soon as they saw the two women come in. Miss Pynchon eyed the table full of gifts.

"I hope you have room in your luggage for all of that." She said it like she was sure Minna didn't.

"I'll make room. I'm leaving all my books here for the children to use."

"Now children, I have gifts for you and then you can run along. I need to take your teacher to the train station."

The children gazed at Miss Pynchon expectantly.

Minna's shoulders drooped. She had hoped to have her goodbyes with the children a bit more private.

Miss Pynchon handed a piece of fruit to each child. They thanked her profusely. Each "*Da-wa-eh*" was met with a stern look and admonishment, "…in English!"

"Thank you!"

"That's better! Honestly, Minerva, sometimes I think they taught you more Indian than you taught them English!"

Minna opened her mouth to protest then thought better of it. *Hah, maybe so…*

Minna moved to the door and the children filed through.

"Goodbye Miss Minna!" they each said in turn. Some of the younger ones hugged her as they went through the door.

Minna bent down to return the hug. "*Dru-we-shots,*" she whispered. She hoped Miss Pynchon did not see her eyes welling up with tears.

After the last child had vacated the schoolroom, Miss Pynchon clapped her hands. "Let's move on!" She said brightly.

Minna turned back for one last look. *Lord, help me to remember…and help me to forget!*

***

Mrs. Salita pulled her shawl up over her head like a canopy. It wasn't comfortable but it offered her some shade from the hot sun.

"Eh-Hiay! I look like a giant bat!"

She paused to look back at how far she had come. She could still see Laguna in the distance.

Not far enough!

She had no intention of walking all the way to Cubero. She knew any minute now someone would come along, take pity on an old woman, and offer her a ride.

The road stretched on before her and behind her. No car in sight. She trudged on.

Should have taken that Miss Pynchon's car! Then I would know they haven't left yet!

Mrs. Salita stopped again and dabbed at her eyes with a handkerchief. She had left them packing that car with Minna's things. She had begged them to wait before they left until she could do one errand. She didn't know what else to do. How long would they wait for her, she wondered?

All my picnic schemes weren't of any use! Bet that Miss Pynchon didn't even ask the school board if Minna could stay! She squared her shoulders and moved on. *I was too subtle! Now the time comes for plain talk. If I can get there in time! Lord, I am wasting time here! Are you going to help me out or not!*

As if in answer, Mrs. Salita heard a rumbling noise and turned to see a logging truck chugging along. It was coming in the right direction! It passed her, then pulled over to the side. A young Indian man jumped out of the cab and waved his hat.

"*Ga-wa-tze,* Naya! What are you doing out here?"

It was Mrs. Rosario's son, Roland!

Eh Hiay! I see you have a sense of humor, Lord! I hope he hasn't been drinking!

Mrs. Salita hurried up to the truck.

"*Ga-wa-tze!* How about you give an old woman a ride?"

"Sure thing." He opened the passenger side door and Mrs. Salita's face fell. *Too high!*

"How am I going to get up there?"

Roland pulled a wooden box from behind the seat and placed it on the ground. Mrs. Salita pulled herself up on the box but it was still too high to reach the seat. She turned back to Roland.

"Roland Rosario if you ever tell your mother about this, I will have to consider the sin of murder!" She bent over the seat as far as she could reach and allowed Roland to shove her back side until her feet could scramble up and into the cab.

Roland slammed the door and then came around the cab to the drivers side, laughing all the way.

He leaped easily into the driver's seat and leaned over to a visibly shaken Mrs. Salita.

"Where to?"

She mopped her face with the handkerchief.

"Cubero! And don't spare the gas!"

They roared off.

Mrs. Salita cranked down the window and gulped air.

Hope I survive this!

They were flying now. She smiled. Just a few more miles!

"Thought you were away at war," she said.

Roland shifted gears and sped up even faster to Mrs. Salita's approval.

"War's over!"

At last the sight of the mission building appeared in the windshield. Mrs. Salita craned her neck to see.

***

Robert swung the sledge hammer with all his strength. The wood broke up with a satisfying crunch. When the volunteer men came out that morning to demolish the rotting porch off the mission, Robert had joined in enthusiastically. It was a good way to let off some steam.

Robert swallowed hard. *Why did you bring her to me, Lord? Okay, okay. Maybe you didn't bring her to me. Maybe you brought her to the children. Then why are you taking her away? I know your ways are always best...but...*

Robert took another swing at the wood, trying not to think what he was thinking. That if he thought Minna cared for him, he would have to go get her and talk her out of marrying her soldier boy.

Her soldier boy! Why didn't he take her back with him when he came to Laguna? There must be something I'm missing here. Maybe she turned him down? All that time she heard nothing from him…I wish I knew for sure! Lord, if you could just find a way to tell me what to do!

"Hadn't you better get over to Laguna to see *Dyety* off?" Albert was picking up debris and carrying it over to a truck bed to be hauled off.

"Say what?"

"*Dyety* leaves today, I heard."

"Today?" Robert felt a wave of panic rising in his chest. "She hasn't asked me for a ride to Santa Fe."

"Naw. That other school lady is taking her."

"Miss Pynchon?"

"Hah, that's the one."

Robert excused himself from the work and hurried inside the building. *No time to clean up properly!* He splashed some water on his face and dusted himself off as he searched for the keys to the toodlelooka.

The men on the roof hollered good naturedly at him as he pulled away from the mission.

Surely she hasn't left yet! Robert pushed the toodlelooka to the limit, pressing the gas pedal to the floor. *Hope I don't get a ticket! Or have an accident!*

He was on the back side of Frog mesa when the toodlelooka coughed, sputtered and gave up the ghost with a cloud of steam pouring out from under the hood.

Have mercy!

Robert opened the car door dejectedly. *Now what?* He paced there on the side of the road for awhile looking east and west. *Not a single vehicle, Lord?*

The mesa loomed above him. *Laguna must be just over that mesa, as the crow flies.*

Robert stood back with mouth agape at the rock wall in front of him. He had been walking for some distance surveying the wall for any kind of foot path leading upward. Now he thought he saw one. It would not be an easy climb, certainly not as easy as the Laguna side, not that the path there was exactly easy. This one would definitely require more exertion.

Some of the rocks looked like steps leading upward. He noted the clay and sandstone layers above him and thought he could see hand and foot holds leading to the top. *May have been how the petroglyph maker went up hundreds, or even a thousand years ago.* Robert scrambled up to the next level practically on hands and knees. He observed how far he had come. *What a lonely place!*

He shaded his gaze with a hand to his eyes. There was a shadow in the sun on the rim of the mesa. Someone was up there!

"Minna?" Robert called. He resumed his efforts and climbed a bit further. No, it wasn't Minna. *How silly of me!* It was a boy looking down on him. It was Amos.

"Move to your left!" The young man shouted. "It's easier there. I'll give you a hand up." Amos ran along the edge and showed the way.

Robert pulled himself over the rim of the mesa and tried to get his bearings.

What a view! As always!

***

"Ga-wa-tse!" Roland called to the men still working on the mission. "Is *Kenuty* around?"

"No." Albert approached Roland and Mrs. Salita. "He's on his way back to Laguna. Didn't you pass him on the road?"

"You want to wait for him here?" Roland asked Mrs. Salita.

"No! I have to find him!" She stopped to consider. *We didn't pass him on the road so he's not headed for Laguna!* She blew her breath out.

"He's not in Laguna!" She moaned. She just didn't know what to do.

"There!" One of the men exclaimed. He was up on top of the mission building. "Is that his automobile I see at the foot of the mesa?"

Roland climbed the ladder and squinted into the sun. "Maybe...yes, I think it is."

"Can you take me that far?" Mrs. Salita asked.

Roland hesitated. "Well, I guess it's not that far. They keep track of my miles on the truck you know, and dock my pay if it is too far off..."

"Roland Rosario!" Mrs. Salita spit out, "Think of all the times Robert has given you a ride and always without any thought of payment!"

Roland considered. "Okay." He said. "I guess I could take you that far. Just this once."

They got back on the logging truck and rumbled off in the direction of the toodlelooka.

***

Robert grasped the outstretched hand Amos offered and scrambled over the lip of the mesa. "Da-wa-eh, son," he said.

"You looking for Miss Minna?"

"Yes, but my automobile isn't cooperating."

"She was up here. I think she left a message for you."

"A message?"

Amos led the way to the bat cave.

***

Roland and Mrs. Salita examined the empty toodlelooka.

"Looks to me like he climbed the mesa." Roland said.

"Eh-hiay! Guess we'll have to go back to Laguna."

Roland poked around under the hood of Robert's automobile. "I think I can fix this."

Mrs. Salita opened the passenger side door with a sigh.

***

Robert didn't even consider going back to his automobile. It would waste valuable time. Quicker to go over the mesa on the

131

Laguna side. He had to see Minna before she left! He had to stop her!

To his horror, when he was about halfway down off the mesa he could see a car pulling away from the schoolhouse.

Please Lord, don't let it be her!

Robert was completely out of breath and red faced when he got to the schoolhouse. He rushed into the schoolroom.

"Minna!"

There were a few children sitting on the folding chairs with their backs to Robert. One child was standing at the front of the room. They were playing "school." The child pretending to be Minna was tugging at her ear. *Just like Minna!* Robert paused briefly with a bittersweet smile. The children had picked up on her deafness. *Her deafness!* It hit Robert like a boulder off a cliff. No wonder she hadn't responded when he told her how he felt about her. He had whispered in her ear. Her deaf ear!

Gasping for breath he stumbled next door to Mrs. Salita's house.

"Mrs. Salita!" He called at the door. When no one answered he opened the door and called again. His heart sinking, he tiptoed into the house, down the hall and into the kitchen. There he spied a note propped up on the sugar bowl on the table.

Dearest Mrs. Salita,

I am sorry I wasn't able to tell you goodbye properly. We waited for you until Miss Pynchon was afraid I would miss my train in Santa Fe. Please tell Robert I am sorry I couldn't wait to say goodbye.

I want to thank you so much for everything you have done for me. The first day I met you I thought everyone called you "Naya" because it was your first name. I have since learned that "Naya" is the word for mother here in Laguna. That is what you have been and will always be to me. Da-wa-eh, Naya! Da-wa-eh!

I love you and will miss you,
Minna Cagle

Robert jogged through the village sure that either his heart or his lungs would burst. Some of the children came after him and jogged alongside, giggling and squealing. Robert scarcely knew they were there. They dropped behind one by one.

At last he reached the main road and turned toward Albuquerque. Surely a car would come along soon. His legs burned with fatigue but he kept up a steady pace, now starting to limp.

The sun was merciless and Robert had to stop, afraid he was about to pass out. *How foolish of me to start out without any water!*

The road ahead of him was swimming and the road behind… *What's that?* A car was approaching. One very much like his own. In fact wasn't that Roland Rosario driving it? And to Robert's amazement he was sure he saw Mrs. Salita's face straining forward in the windshield. It was the last thing he saw before he passed out.

***

Minna gave up trying to hear what Miss Pynchon was saying. She had been in constant chatter ever since they left Laguna. With the top down on the convertible and the road noise in competition, there was just no way to make it out.

It didn't much matter, Minna realized, as she pulled a scarf over her wind tangled hair. She almost smiled at the thought of finally turning a "deaf ear" to Esmae Pynchon.

When they arrived at the train station in Santa Fe Minna was already exhausted. When her luggage was taken care of, she and Miss Pynchon found themselves in an awkward state of goodbyes.

"Well, this is it then," Miss Pynchon said matter of factly.

"Yes. It is."

"Oh, I thought I'd give you a little something as a goodbye and good luck gift." Miss Pynchon handed her a brown paper wrapped box. "I noticed you admired these and so I thought you should have them."

"Thank you, Miss Pynchon."

"So, goodbye then."

"Goodbye."

Miss Pynchon shook Minna's hand. Pulling on her white gloves, she left in a hurry.

Minna boarded the locomotive and sat down wearily on the seat by the window. She half heartedly pulled off the brown wrapper and lifted the lid to the box. It was the shoes Miss Pynchon had worn the day of Gloria and Leon's wedding. They were somewhat scuffed but still useable.

Minna slipped off her own shoes and exchanged them for the heels. She was surprised to see that they fit perfectly.

Well, then no more need for the cardboard for awhile. Minna reached inside the old shoe and pulled out the last piece of cardboard she had used to plug the hole. It was Frank's picture. She slowly ripped it to many small pieces. *Won't be needing this anymore!* It was very satisfying.

Minna sighed heavily and leaned her weary head against the window.

***

Robert fought his way back to the surface of consciousness. Mrs. Salita was patting his cheeks when he opened his eyes. Roland handed her a canteen of water and she tipped it up to Robert's lips.

"I'm sorry, *Kenuty*. It must have been a shock seeing us borrowing your car."

"What happened?"

"Roland didn't want to bring the truck back so I figured if we borrowed your car we could meet up with you in Laguna. That is where you have been, right?"

Robert sat up straighter. "Minna!"

"Yes, she has left already with Miss Pynchon."

"I have to get to Santa Fe!"

"Well, let's go then!"

Mrs. Salita and Roland each took an arm and they helped Robert to the toodlelooka.

"I don't know if you should drive, Robert." Roland looked anxiously back toward Cubero. "I'll drive if you want."

Settled in the front seat next to Roland, Robert mopped his face with his handkerchief. He still felt a little woozy. He murmured out loud, "I wonder if that hand on the cave wall meant Minna just hoped to marry in general or that she still plans to marry Frank?"

"Marry Frank?" Mrs. Salita looked at Robert like she thought he had lost his mind. Robert shook his head. He hadn't meant to say it out loud.

Mrs. Salita scoffed, "What are you babbling about Robert? Frank is already married!" Robert nearly passed out again in shock.

"Already married? Is that what he came to tell her a week ago?"

"Eh-hiay, Robert! I thought you knew, that was Minna's brother."

"Her brother?" Robert held back tears of frustration. "I had everything wrong! Can we go any faster?" Roland grinned with amusement as he shifted gears. "Hold on to something!"

Just as they pulled into the Santa Fe station, they heard the whistle. *Please don't let me miss her!*

Robert leaped out of the toodlelooka. "Minna!" He yelled as he came around the building. Roland and Mrs. Salita followed. Robert frantically searched all the windows he could see on the locomotive.

"All Aboard!" The conductor yelled.

There she is!

"Minna!" Robert jumped up as high as he could under the window. Finally he thumped it on the last leap. Minna's face turned to look out.

"Minna! Don't leave! I love you!" Robert yelled.

Her face looked out but with no understanding.

"What?" she mouthed. She pointed to her ear and shook her head. Robert looked frantically around. How to make her understand? There was nothing!

Then he saw a man white washing the adobe station walls.

Robert leaped over two suitcases and plunged his hand right into the bucket of paint. Rushing back to the locomotive he jumped up and slapped the window, leaving a chalky white handprint there.

The petroglyph! Understanding brightened Minna's face. She jumped up and soon appeared on the exit stairs.

Minna!" Robert yelled. "Don't go! Come back with me. I want you to be my wife!"

Minna leaped from the steps into his arms. He swung her around, both of them laughing.

Roland nudged Mrs. Salita. "Well, isn't that something?"

Mrs. Salita nodded her tear streaked face. "*Hah*! Something!"

THIRTEEN

Laguna
December 1

Dear David,

Thank you so very much for your letter. It was wonderful, only of course I'm disappointed that you can't get to come to my wedding. It would be so much fun to introduce you to all our Indian friends and I would have been so proud of you as my best man. But thank you for wanting to come and thank you for the check. It will surely come in handy on this occasion, and I hope I will be seeing all of you in the not too distant future. Is it all right to show your letter to Minna? It better be, because I yammergonta before you have a chance to stop me. She will be tickled almost to death.

You asked if "Minna" was a nickname. Yes, her given name is Minerva, but she doesn't like to be called that. Here at Laguna they call her "Dyety" which means rabbit. They think she wiggles her nose and lips just like a rabbit when she eats. It is so endearing.

We plan to get married on the 15ᵗʰ of December. Wish you could be here, all of you in fact. It will be wonderful to be with you at Christmas, the first time in seven years. Until then, best wishes and 'hallucinations'!

Your Loving Brother,
Robert

Minna stood at the back of the mission room and smoothed the skirt to her new white suit. She thought it looked nice with Miss Pynchon's shoes, but walking around the building had made them dusty. She hastily stood on one leg and dusted one shoe off on the back of her stockings, then changing feet, did the same for the other.

It was a wonderful turnout. All of their friends were there. Gloria and Leon looked back and smiled at her. Emma and Roland sat next to them and right up front were Mrs. Salita, Albert, and Albert's mother sitting together!

The mission board had come through with a wonderful wedding present, a pump organ for the mission. They had even sent someone to play it for this occasion. Minna looked forward to learning to play when she returned from the wedding trip.

Miss Betty Smith saw Minna standing at the back and as arranged, began playing "Savior, Like A Shepherd Lead Us." Dr. Anderson, Superintendent of Indian Missions took front center to officiate and Robert joined him. He was sporting a brand new suit, courtesy of his brother's generous check. He looked so proud with his shoulders back and shining face. His brother, Sam, took his place next to him and Minna's brother Ernest Leigh also stood up. The two brothers were wearing their military uniforms.

Minna reached up to touch the little bouquet of posies pinned in her hair and stepped forward. She could hear the people whispering as she walked down the aisle. She understood some of it with the little Keresan she knew. They were expressing their approval. She beamed.

When she arrived next to Robert they both turned to face Dr. Anderson.

"Hello, Minna," Robert whispered.

"Hello, Robert. How're you holdin' up?" she answered.

"I'm finer'n frog's hair!"

Dr. Anderson opened his Bible to Ephesians 5:20-33 and read the passage concerning husbands and wives.

Minna turned her good ear to him but found it hard to catch everything he said. He had the habit of starting every sentence loud and trailing off to a whisper at each sentence end.

They came to the part of the ceremony where they would exchange rings. Robert and Minna took hands. The rings lay on top of Dr. Anderson's open Bible. He indicated Minna should take Robert's ring in her hand.

"Repeat after me," he said.

"With this ring, I thee wed…"

Minna leaned in closer.

"What?" she whispered.

Dr. Anderson reacted in surprise but repeated himself.

"With this ring, I thee wed…"

Minna shook her head in confusion.

"What?" she repeated.

Robert's eyes widened. He said through smiling teeth, "He said, With this ring, I thee wed."

"Oh!" Minna blew out a breath of air and said loudly, "WITH THIS RING, I BEWARE!"

***

Mrs. Salita could not contain her tears of joy. She stood in the crowd of friends shouting best wishes to the happy couple. Albert was by her side. She sniffed, "Well, you old Tom cat, we did it!"

Some men were helping Robert push the toodlelooka in reverse so that he and Minna could leave on their honeymoon.

Albert laughed loudly.

"*Hah!* We did!"

A cheer went up from the crowd as the toodlelooka pulled forward. It had been decorated with toilet paper streamers and Minna's old shoes rattled from the bumper. There was a sign propped up in the rear window:

JUST MARRIED
NO SMOKING

She giat-shro yus, ga-ma nye-sih tse-yu-kuh
(And I shall dwell in the house of the Lord forever.)

139

www.ingramcontent.com/pod-product-compliance
Lightning Source LLC
Chambersburg PA
CBHW022025170626
46808CB00003B/1057